Travis I. Sivart

Silver & Smith and the Jazeer's Light

Travis I. Sivart

Silver & Smith and the Jazeer's Light

Book 1 of The Silver & Smith Chronicles

Cover Design by Travis I. Sivart

Edited by Tara Moeller

DreamPunk Press

ISBN: 978-1-954214-58-3

Travis I. Sivart

Enjoying what you're reading?
Want some more for free?

Go to TravisSivart.com/work

Travis I. Sivart

Dedication

Let's raise a glass and toast the heroes that have always made us feel better about ourselves; Indiana Jones, Captain Jack Sparrow, Sherlock Holmes (RDJ), Star-Lord, and so many others.

Table of Contents

Silver & Smith and the Jazeer's Light

Travis I. Sivart

Chapter 1

Silver's vision swam. He pushed himself to go on, deeper into the two-thousand-year-old tomb. A dragon's egg awaited.

The LED light in his hands flickered and Silver licked his lips, sweat beading on his forehead. The metallic taste in his mouth and the slight loss of equilibrium passed; he attributed it to the depth underground, and the many corroded bronze and copper pipes, statues, and artifacts surrounding him in the tomb.

Silver was tall with a runner's build, and his dark skin and dark clothes blended with the shadows. Only the silver accents of various buckles, snaps, and clips stood out. Even his various weapons were jet black. He wiped his sweaty palms on his black shirt and then on the thighs of his black pants.

"What was that?" asked Pepper from beside him, smacking his lips and rubbing his temple.

Garry Pepper was head and shoulders shorter than Silver, but spoke with the bravado of a larger man. He swaggered as he walked, wiping dust from his shaved head. His outfit was simple, but military in style.

"Shh, Garry," Silver's voice was low, and he hunched to duck under the overhead pipes, "we need to listen, not talk. These tombs are dangerous, and any sound could warn us of a trap being sprung."

"I've been a Commander in the SIS for a decade," Garry said, walking under the obstruction without ducking, "and in the organization since the restructure in 2020 after the Brexit fiasco, and never seen a terracotta army, dodged traps set a couple thousand years ago, or found myself dizzy around a bald guy before."

"Garry, we're both bald," Silver leaned his shoulder against a corner and peeked around it, "now be quiet before someone hears us."

"Mate, no one is following us and nothing living has been down here in a couple of millennia. I think we're going to be ok," Garry snorted and leaned on the opposite wall as he looked Silver over. "Unless your super-bright flashlight reflecting off my pale skin attracts some mystical beast from eons past. That's what you say happened the last time, right, Silver?"

"That wasn't in this place, and one's different. That was in the catacombs where I found the coded tile sequence that I'll need to open the egg's hidden compartment in the throne room ahead," Silver checked the cardphone on his wrist bracer, making sure the air they were breathing hadn't soured, "and remember, Garry, you insisted on joining me for this, and I still have no idea why."

"Government regulations and all that," Garry looked over his companion's shoulder, "don't you think the flashlight will give you away to anything in the next room?"

The tall man ignored his British companion and spun around the corner, crouching. Pivoting on his heels, Silver scanned the room for any threats.

Once he made sure the room was clear, he stood. Moving along the wall, he turned the flashlight towards the center of the room.

A dozen columns, six on each side of the room,

rose to the height of five men, a layer of dust muting the color of the creamy jade inlay on each of them. The floor-to-ceiling mosaics told the story of how dragons came to this world, and later left, each pillar telling another piece of tale and recounting battles, heroes, and significant events in this piece of history that was now classified as mythology.

Silver wondered if it was actual history. Had things existed in this world that people no longer believed possible?

This wasn't the first time that this idea had crossed his mind. He'd spent weeks tracking information about so many pieces of history and the artifacts associated with them as he haunted the rooftops of Hong Kong, hidden among the steel pipes, whining drones zipping through the air, and the haze of pollution.

Dressed as a gang member—including the tapering Asian coolie hat, a fluttering shoulder capelet, and a chain on the katana-like blade he'd carried—the bounty hunter had followed and watched street level thugs, buying and bullying information. In silk suits, he'd followed and watched corporate thugs, buying and bullying information. It amazed him that two worlds, so different, were so alike.

Shaking the thoughts away, he focused on the layout of the room.

The columns were thick enough that Garry and Silver could barely encircle one if they held hands. They created a path down the center of the chamber, a tarnished bronze gong as tall as a man hanging in front of the nearest wall. An immense marble throne with emerald and gold inlay sat at the other end of the hall. The gong and the throne were each on their own raised dais.

The musty smell of stagnant water permeated the air, and the sound of a steady dripping broke the silence. The men's footfalls echoed off the intricately carved ceramic floor tiles.

"Stay near the walls," Silver motioned Garry away from the center of the floor, "there's a better chance of triggering a trap in the middle—like you did in the other room—than against the walls."

"That was a fluke, and you know it. The falling rocks that did it, not me." Garry gestured towards the raised gong, "How about I just stay over here then? That way, at least one of us will survive this adventure."

Creeping along, one hand on the wall, Silver set each foot down with care. He paused, listening for anything that sounded like a trap being triggered.

When he was even with the last pillar in front of the throne, Silver braced one leg against the wall and faced the center of the room. Pushing off the wall, he leapt across the floor, landing on the base of the marble and jade column, hugging it to keep from stepping backwards.

Reorienting himself so he was facing the Emperor's Dais, he lined up his next jump. Silver bounded across the space to land, catlike, on the steps.

The sound of ancient rusting gears popped, spears thrusting forward from the stone arms of the ruler's chair. Silver spun to the center of the platform and jumped onto the throne. Metal spikes sprung upward from the steps as the limber man leapt out of their path and landed on the stone seat.

Silver looked down, fingering the slash in his black graphene sleeve where a spear had caught. Blood welled from the wound. The thin armored material could stop the bullets of the rebels in the forest they crossed to get here, but a blade would slice through it as easily as any other cloth.

Silver turned back to his task. He ran his hand across the raised runes on the chair's left arm, caressing the ancient text with reverence.

He raised his left arm and checked his cardphone—verifying the code he'd recovered from the catacombs—and pressed tiles on the throne in a matching sequence. Clicks and whirrs issued from under the seat of power. A sigh of air escaped from hidden crevasses and holes in the room.

"The traps are disarmed," Silver's deep baritone echoed around the room. "Feel free to move about the cabin."

"Yep," Garry's voice sounded thin and reedy compared to Silver's. The smaller man moved towards the gong, inspecting it with his flashlight. "Got it. Carry on and get the mystical, magical, dragon baby."

"It's just an egg," Silver moved his long, delicate fingers across the right arm of the chair, "and bronze at that. Dragons never existed, at least not in this world."

"Are you suggesting that they may exist on other planets?" Garry's voice echoed in the chamber as he ran a hand down the padded mallet that hung beside the bronze circle. He picked it up and held it in both hands.

"It's a possibility," Silver pressed a series of buttons resembling mahjong tiles, and a stone plate popped up from the arm of the immense chair, "but more likely in other realities."

"You know that the Hubble Group Array has found more evidence of the possibility of life on other planets," Garry inspected the Jiaguwen script on the mallet, "than the CERN LHC—you know, that Large Hadron Collider out in Switzerland—has found for other realities, right?"

"For now," Silver pulled the plate up, revealing a cavity below it, "but who knows what'll happen in the future?"

"Are you talking about the ILC, the International Linear Collider?" Garry laughed, turning towards Silver, holding the mallet in one hand and shining his flashlight at the mercenary. "That forty-billion-dollar monstrosity hasn't shown any results since they turned it on two years ago and has had more issues than the original."

"They do have a third one in the planning stages." Silver lifted a large greenish-yellow ovoid from the arm, bringing it to his chest with care, hesitating when it clanked against his harness and the attached pouches.

"No one knows what the future holds," Garry shrugged and turned back towards the gong.

"Some know more than others." Silver stepped off the seat of the throne and onto the floor. Seeing Garry hefting the mallet, he stopped in his tracks. "What are you doing, Garry?"

"Just seeing what this does," Garry laughed, swinging the mallet at the gong, striking it hard.

"No!" Silver rushed forward, one arm stretched towards Garry, who was half a football field away.

The tinny sound reverberated through the room, echoing off the stone walls, floor, and ceiling.

The sound of cracking stone devoured Silver's dismayed cry.

The walls crumbled, exposing grinding pulleys and ropes. Stones hit the floor, creating holes, and the meter-wide floor tiles spun sideways and fell into the abyss beneath them. Crossbeams supporting the floor spun downward into the inky black, leaving only the two daises at each end of the chamber.

The floor fell away from the throne first, leaving the massive chair on a floating island at the end of the room. Cradling the egg with both arms, Silver ran forward, jumping from tile to tile, his foot leaving one a second before it fell into the darkness.

Bounding from collapsing tile to falling beam, Silver tucked the egg under one arm and grabbed a knife from a sheath on his thigh.

Stabbing it into a pillar, he used it as a handhold and pushed off the column with his feet, launching himself three paces to the next stone support.

Landing on a falling tile, he dropped into the pit. He released his flashlight, letting it spin downwards, circles of light illuminating the endless drop. Pushing upwards, he grabbed the thin shelf that the floor tiles had rested on jutting out of the last pillar with his fingertips. Dangling, he searched for a way to pull himself up without dropping the ancient treasure.

"Throw it to me!" Garry shouted.

Silver looked at Garry, who stood with his arms wide, flashlight at his feet, leaning out over the precipice towards Silver.

"Why the hell did you bang the gong?" Silver slowly turned his body, struggling to keep his grip.

"Do you think I knew what would happen?" Garry laughed. "Do you think I had any clue that it was a deadman's switch that would do all this?"

Silver's eyes narrowed.

"Just throw me the egg," Garry leaned further over, "and then I can throw you a rope so we can both get out of here."

Silver looked around for another way, glancing at the straps of his knapsack on his shoulder. He could hear distant stone collapsing, ropes and pulleys creaking back as they reset.

"You'll never get your rucksack off your back without dropping the egg or falling." Garry sighed, standing up and crossing his arms. "Just throw me the egg, so we have a chance of it getting back up to the world, or risk both of us being lost forever."

Silver nodded and dropped his free arm. Garry gasped as the egg fell, landing in Silver's open hand. Swinging his arm upward, the mercenary tossed the invaluable artifact underhand to the military agent.

Garry leaned forward, catching the egg with both hands, his weight balanced on the balls of his feet, swaying at the edge of the precipice. He fell back on his heels and dropped to the floor on his butt.

"You did that on purpose," Garry snarled.

"Do you think I had any clue that it would do that?" Silver reached up with his free hand, grabbing the tiny ledge with the fingertips of both hands. "Throw me a rope, and let's get out of here."

"Right, about that," a smug smile spread across Garry's face, "Central Command said the fewer folks that know about this, the better. And since you're just hired muscle, you're disposable. An acceptable loss. But England thanks you for your services."

"Garry," Silver gritted his teeth, looking around for another way to safety, "I'll see a bullet in your head if you're serious, and will beat you within a centimeter of your life if you're just messing with me. Throw me a rope."

"Silver," Garry sighed, turning to leave, "you always were crap with people. Have a good life."

Whistling "God Save the King" Commander Garry Pepper tucked the egg under his arm, bent and retrieved his electric torch, and walked into the dark tunnel that led out. The creaking noise of the booby trap grew louder, and the floor between the gong and exit collapsed behind the man.

Silver stared at his employer and partner's receding back and the circle of light that highlighted Garry's silhouette. Once the room was completely dark, the mercenary blinked out the activation code for his multi-vision lenses. The contacts cycled through their settings until landing on the infrared-lowlight combo. Garry's fading heat signature dimmed as Silver looked in the direction the man had gone.

Holding on with his right hand, Silver reached down to his left thigh and grabbed a cylinder about the length of his hand from a pocket. Aiming in the direction of the wall behind the gong, he pressed a button on the side of the cylinder. A steel dart, with filament attached, launched across the space, the cord unwinding behind. Garry's distant laugh played a discordant melody to the harmony of the resounding noise of the gong being struck. It echoed throughout the room for a second time. Silver heard rushing liquid in the copper pipes as he triggered another trap. The cord went limp, slipping into the chasm.

Winding the cord back into the handle with the press of a button, Silver tried again. This time it struck the stone of the support beside the gong, biting into it. Holding the small baton against the pillar in front of him, Silver pressed another button and an anchor spike shot out with a puff of compressed air, penetrating the stone.

Releasing his grip on the pillar, his fingers cramping,

he gripped the baton with both hands. Sliding a switch on the steel shaft, the baton slid upward along the filament line with a mechanical whir, carrying Silver towards the gong.

His contacts showed the cooler stone coming closer, and he swung his legs up, clearing the floor of the platform before he hit it.

Letting go of the steel shaft, he laid on his back on the cold rock floor for a moment, rubbing his hands until feeling returned. Sitting up, he assessed the situation.

Pulling a small square box from a pouch, he clipped the light to his harness and flicked it to life, blinking the code to return his contacts to normal.

Silver grabbed the steel baton, and with a few presses of buttons, released the steel tips, reset new ones, retracted the cord, and set it up to use again.

Moments later, now across the chasm and in the hall leading out, he reset the device again and stowed it. He jogged down the hall towards the exit, caution discarded in his need to catch up to Garry.

The thin copper pipes dripped faster now, the liquid hissing when it hit the wood support beams that held the walls and ceiling in place. The acrid smell permeated the air and Silver picked up his pace, wary of what that may mean.

A mist issued from a pipe ahead. Slowing to look, Silver noted the small clogged holes alternating on the underneath or side of the pipes every meter. The pressure of the liquid in the pipes was clearing more of the openings every few moments. With small popping noises, more of the pungent liquid sprayed into the tunnel ahead and behind him.

Reaching out with a hand and watching the vapor

land on his glove, Silver saw the material becoming etched.

"Acid," Silver muttered, "it's old, but…"

Silver broke into a run.

At his top speed, the mercenary took corners with reckless abandon, staying to the far side of the tunnel wherever the acid had cleared the plugged holes in the pipes. He dodged streams, sprays, and fogs of the flesh-eating liquid, running headlong down the only route to freedom.

Cracking came from above, and a waterfall of the harsh liquid spilled from the ceiling on his left. Dirt sprinkled down around him, a stray draft giving him a temporary reprieve from the harsh smell.

Increasing his speed, Silver pressed against the wall to get past the flow, holding one arm up to block as much as he could.

Now, at a dead sprint, bouncing off the sides of the tunnel as he took corners, ducking, Silver broke into the main chamber housing the terracotta army of Emperor Qin Shi Huang.

A bullet ricocheted off the compacted dirt next to Silver's head as light flooded the room.

Chapter 2

"You *just* don't give up, do you?" Garry's forehead creased and his lip pulled back in a sneer. "Why can't you just quit?"

"I try to keep calm and carry on, you know?" Silver straightened, shaded his eyes from the bright lights, and looked around.

Garry was to Silver's right, in the passageway's opening that led to the surface. To the left, in the excavated pits of the mausoleum, thousands of terracotta soldiers and hundreds of ceramic horses stood in neat rows.

A half dozen frameworks with LED lights were angled around the site, casting enormous shadows away from the two men. Silver stood in the newest passage—rivulets of acid trickling between his boots—dug out by himself and Garry hours before.

"Don't get cheeky with me," Garry leveled his weapon at Silver, "this is done. I was just hoping to not have to do it myself."

"Because you're a coward and don't have the balls to do the hard things?" Silver raised his eyebrows and tilted his head. "Or is it because you wouldn't be able to sleep tonight?"

"You really don't know how to talk to people, do you?" Garry aimed down the sight of the pistol. "Especially when they're holding your life in their hands."

"You're going to kill me either way," Silver took a

balanced stance, spreading his legs shoulder-width apart, "and I'd rather die spitting in your face than licking your boots."

Garry clicked the hammer back.

Silver spun to the left and ran, zigzagging towards the army of clay statues.

The surrounding dirt and clay muffled the shot's echo.

Silver threw himself down and slid on his hip between the rows of the pottery soldiers.

When he came to a stop, he glanced down his torso and legs, patting at himself, mentally searching for the pain that should accompany a gunshot.

"You can come out now," a lilting, softer voice said. "The bad man won't be bothering you anymore. Never much trusted the military, anyway."

Silver sat up, and not finding an entry or exit wound, realized he hadn't been shot. He stood and peeked around the statues to see who had saved him.

"That's it," a sandy-haired young woman adjusted her beige vest, fiddling with the many pockets on it as Silver looked between the man-shaped artifacts. Dipping the muzzle of a high-powered rifle, she beckoned him closer. "Come on out now, it's safe."

Silver moved with caution, keeping a statue between him and the newcomer.

"You're a shy one, aren't you?" She tilted the brim of her boonie hat up, smiling a crooked smile. "I'm Hank Smith, an archeologist. And I think we're on the same side."

"Hank is a…" Silver began.

"Yes," Hank swatted at an orange clay stain on the leg of her khaki cargo pants, "it's a boy's name. It's short for Henry."

"But Henry is also a…" Silver started.

"Yeah," Hank interrupted, putting a hand on her hip, and the muzzle of the rifle raising just a tad. "A boy's name. It's short for Henrietta. But I prefer Hank, ok? Is there a problem with that?"

"No, I don't have any issue with your name, who you are, or what you do," the corner of Silver's mouth twitched upward, and he realized he needed to steer the conversation in a different direction before he got himself shot. "Speaking of which, what do you do and what stroke of luck brought you here?"

"Archaeology. Been hunting that thing for months." Hank gestured at the satchel that held the egg and lay next to Garry's crumpled body, blood trickling from the hole in the dead man's temple. "We've been following you for a while now, trying to make sure anything you recovered—or liberated, or whatever you want to call it—ended up where it belongs…in a museum for everyone to appreciate."

"That belongs to my employer," Silver said, nodding towards the bag.

"Oh, you mean this guy?" She nudged the corpse at her feet with the toe of her boot. "This guy who probably wanted it for selfish reasons? Maybe to blackmail another government? Or a gift for some rich benefactor, so they support the next war or election? It doesn't look like he was going to pay you, anyway. Do you still want to stick with the story that it's his?"

Hank placed the butt of her rifle on her hip and stared at Silver. She had followed this man, well, followed his trail, across three countries for the past month. He was a capable foe and was dangerous to cross. Her research on him showed he rarely failed any job he took.

Silver watched the young woman in front of him. She had the high ground, a weapon in her hand, and had saved him. If she had wanted him dead, it would have happened already. Also, she felt good, as in right and well meaning.

Silver shook his head slowly.

Hank let out a breath she hadn't realized she'd been holding.

"You're a pretty good shot with that," he nodded at the rifle. "Where'd you learn to use it?"

"Doesn't matter," Hank said too quickly, too defensively, making Silver think many people questioned her and made her feel as if she had to defend who she was. "I learned it, and that's all that you need to worry about. I'm fast in addition to accurate, so don't try anything. They used to call me the Hawk—back in my school days—because I could spot a target from a damn sight further than anyone else. Keep in mind, you aren't far enough away that I even need to squint. Any more questions?"

The woman's short tirade surprised Silver. He'd meant his comment and question as a compliment, showing respect for her skill with the weapon. She'd taken it as a personal attack, and shut down further conversation about the topic. Silver noted that and kept his distance.

"Yeah," Silver moved his hand to his belt, noticing movement behind Hank. "You said 'we' have been following me. Who is 'we'?"

"Oh, myself and my partner," Hank moved to one side and a tall woman stepped from the shadows of the tunnel behind her, "Joan."

The newcomer glared at Silver and tucked a stray dark hair back into the tight bun on the top of her head.

Her bare arms showed dirt up to where her shirt sleeves had been torn off. Resting one hand on the butt of her Ruger, she leaned on the wall with the other.

"She's a master tracker," Hank continued, "on foot or virtually, and handles the business side of things. Joan Williams, this is…"

"Silver," he said, stepping out from behind the statues.

"Oh geez, Hank," Joan pulled her firearm from its holster, and swung the butt towards Hank's head, "you just never shut the hell up, do you?"

Hank turned to see the gun collide with her face, hard. The blonde woman's head jerked back, and she collapsed to the floor, unconscious.

"Stupid girl is smart, but will never get anywhere in this business," Joan looked down at Hank, and kicked the unconscious woman in the ribs.

Silver moved, drawing Joan's attention.

Joan swung the weapon towards Silver, who dove behind the row of pottery soldiers again. Gunfire cracked and the head of an earthenware warrior exploded.

Landing face first in the dirt, Silver rolled onto his back, pulling throwing knives from his harness.

Why the hell does everyone have a gun except me? Silver thought, rising to a crouch and peeking towards the only exit. *And why did I give mine up before entering the country, and trust Garry to have a spare?*

"Enjoy your tomb, moron," Joan shouted over her shoulder, striding up the dirt passage, gun in one hand and the satchel with the dragon's egg in the other.

Hank lay on the ground at the foot of the ramp, next to the SIS agent she'd killed.

Silver ran forward as Joan disappeared around the

corner. Leaping over the prone forms of his dead partner and the younger woman, he sprinted up the tunnel.

An explosion threw Silver backwards, a cloud of dust and hot air rushing out of the passage as he landed next to Hank, on top of Garry. Dirt and rocks cascaded around them as the shaft out collapsed.

Scrambling backwards, Silver grabbed the girl's arm and dragged her after him. The strap from her rifle entangled her other arm, and the barrel of the weapon snagged on the stones of the floor.

Silver stumbled at the unexpected resistance, yanked Hank's arm, lost his grip, and fell backwards.

Hank moaned, breathing in a mouthful of ceiling. Coughing and hacking, she rolled to her side, pulling her rifle under her as she attempted to spit out what she'd just inhaled.

"Come on," Silver pushed himself to his feet, grabbed her arm and pulled her up to stand beside him as she tried to catch her breath and clear her mouth of dirt. "I have a plan."

"Dude," Hank gasped, "I'm dying here. Let me catch my breath."

"Catch it while we run," Silver wrapped an arm around her waist and lifted her, moving forward, "otherwise we'll both be dying. That damn passage is a goner already."

"What happened?" Hank pushed away from Silver's grasp, stumbling. "And I can run fine all by myself."

"Fine, then run. Follow me, but watch out for the acid." Silver moved back into the tunnel he'd come from a few minutes before, stepping around the corrosive rivulets. "Your girl Joan blew up the tunnel, collapsing the whole thing on top of you. Guessing you weren't too close?"

Hank supported herself with one hand on the wall, following the dark-skinned man deeper into the underground complex.

Silver must be wrong, she thought, *Joan couldn't have done that. She's my friend and partner. She wouldn't have done this.* Looking around as they moved into the dimly lit tunnel, dust dancing across the passage, the truth sank in.

"No, no, no…" Hank muttered, "this is a priceless site, the tomb of the first Emperor of China, there's no other like it."

Glancing over her shoulder, Hank raised her voice so Silver could hear her. "Did I mention Joan is also a demolition expert? How could she do this to a wonder like this?"

"Looks like we were both betrayed by someone we trusted," Silver slowed, angling his flashlight upwards to find where he'd felt the breeze earlier. "par for the course, though."

"My head hurts. Am I rambling?" Hank paused, looking around, then moved forward to catch up. "Where are you leading us? There are no exits this way."

"There wasn't," Silver jabbed at the ceiling with his blades. Soil fell in clods at their feet. "But I think there may be one now, thanks to the booby traps."

The two of them pulled themselves from the crevasse in the earth, spitting dirt and swearing. Blinking in the waning daylight, Silver looked back. Hushing Hank, he pointed at the growing crowd a half kilometer away, near the entrance to the tomb.

"They look angry." Silver kept his voice and body low.

"Can you blame them?" Hank spat, sitting on the ground and smearing the wet loam from her clothes. "The resting place of one of their country's greatest heroes and leaders was just desecrated and possibly destroyed. I'm not even a native, but I'd be ready to kill someone with my bare hands if I caught them anywhere near here."

"You mean like Joan?" Silver asked.

Hank just grunted.

"Then maybe we should be a bit less conspicuous about our presence here?" Silver moved away, crouching.

"Oh," Hank covered her mouth, eyes wide at the realization of danger, "yeah, I guess so."

Hank shouldered her rifle and scrambled to catch up to her newly acquired guide.

"It's a shame we're leaving empty-handed," she said when she caught up.

"Who says we are?" Silver held up a jade stamp. "I happened to pick up the He Shi Bi when rummaging through Qin Shi Huang's junk drawer."

"You found the Emperor's lost seal?" Hank stopped in her tracks. "That's been missing since the tenth century."

"Yes," Silver looked over his shoulder, a sly grin splitting his face, "but not anymore. And we should keep moving before we bring half the province down on us."

"Where are we going?" she whispered.

"We're going east," Silver muttered, "then I'm going back to London."

"London is nice this time of year," Hank glanced back over her shoulder to make sure the growing mob hadn't spotted them.

"Don't you have somewhere else to go? London's always miserable; rain, tourists, traffic, angry drunks." Silver turned south, heading for a safe house he'd set up.

"Naw," Hank moved to walk beside her new travelling companion and slapped him on the shoulder, "I don't mind all those things, just more folks with interesting stories. I think I'll tag along and keep you company."

"You do what you need to do." Silver eyed her sideways. "But first, we have a train to catch."

Chapter 3

"Croaker, I don't need a little brother, a roommate, a dog, a cat, a painted box turtle, or anything else," Silver said into the receiver of his cardphone. "I like my place clean and quiet."

"Fine," said a voice that sounded like it had been gargling gravel for half a century, "but if you're not careful, you'll end up like me."

"Well traveled?" Silver said, leaning forward and picking up his glass of water.

"You don't know the half of it," Croaker laughed.

"Half is about all I know," the conversation lulled as Silver took a deep drink. "So, do you have a line on a job or not?"

"Yeah, I do. It's with the Royal British Museum. And before you say no, I want to point out that the museum isn't a part of the actual government. I know you're once bitten, twice shy, considering what you just went through."

"Let me think about it," Silver sighed, leaning back on his grey couch, and tossing the cardphone onto the table in front of him. He could hear Croaker puffing on a pipe through the speakers in the room.

Dust danced in the ray of sunlight intruding on his third-floor flat in downtown London, pressing through the vertical blinds and the graphene window treatments. Three layers; the first layer was two molecules thick to prevent bullets from piercing the window, the second layer was wired to the solar collector, and the third layer could be clear, opaque, or have his computer screen projected through it.

Standing and wandering around the apartment, Silver shuffled through the three pieces of mail on the counter. The place was simple, with a bedroom and bathroom on one side of the living room, and the kitchen and dining room combined on the other side. The bar where he usually ate his meals overlooked the small living room. Staring at the metal appliances in the kitchen, he made a mental note to call the cleaning service to dust.

"Did you think about it yet?" Croaker's voice interrupted Silver's thoughts.

"It's only been a minute and a half," Silver stretched, tapping at the beam in the center of the ceiling.

"Yeah," Croaker slurped from his drink, making Silver cringe at the noise, "and I'm bored. Do you want the job or not?"

"Yes," Silver heaved another sigh, "why not? When and where?"

Hank whistled, placing the trinket she'd picked up at the junk shop in Lintong District on a shelf, adjusting the half dozen other knick-knacks around it to make room.

Stepping back, she scanned the four wall units and admired her collection.

"You know," Hank said to no one in particular, "the bright yellow wall behind it really does make these treasures pop when you look at them."

A sleek, black cat pressed against her leg and let

out a raucous meow.

"Oh Frick, I know you like the lavender of the dining room better," she bent to scratch the cat's head, "and if you keep this up, Frack will get all jealous."

Glancing at Frack, the ginger cat glaring at her through slitted eyes from the kitchen counter—where she wasn't supposed to be—Hank smiled and stood up.

Whistling again, she moved to the counter and patted Frack, who growled even as she purred. Frick still wound himself around Hank's legs.

"Darcy," Hank shouted to her roommate, "I'm going to the café. Can I bring you anything back?"

"No thanks," came a voice from one of the back rooms. "I'm going out in a bit. Be home late, so don't wait up with cocoa and popcorn again, ok?"

"No promises!" Hank laughed.

Moving around Frick to the kitchen table, Hank fluffed the fresh daisies there, and then picked up her lunch dishes.

Depositing the plate, glass, and flatware in the sink, she turned and typed a few items into the grocery tablet on the fridge. She pressed send so it would deliver the list to both her and Darcy's phones.

Shouting a goodbye to Darcy, Hank grabbed her keycard and cardphone, and pushed them into a pocket. She moved Frick away from her legs with one foot and slipped out the front door.

Five flights down, she chatted with her landlady for a few minutes before heading outside. This was one of the streets that had been 'reclaimed', meaning car traffic was prohibited and people could sit on benches, stroll along the street, sunbathe, or even paint in the road if they liked.

Hank detoured into a corner shop, chatting with the shopkeeper about his wife's surgery as she bought a pack of gum and some mints.

After that, she swung by the café for her favorite drink; a plain black coffee. It was an affection she'd picked up from being on dig sites. Dark coffee was always available, but the rich, full-bodied stuff that was boiled until it burned was not. She loved it. The barista behind the counter with all their piercings, tattoos, and glib stories about the characters in the tube on the way to and from work kept her chatting for long enough to order a second cup.

An hour later, Hank was on her way to work. It was about time she faced the music after filing her report about what happened in China.

Silver sat at the bar of The Cask & Custard Pot. The pub had a rich history of punk music and bar brawls until it was bought out and cleaned up by Kevin, the tall, thin man behind the bar. The place was done in a classic dark wood décor, and a huge stone fireplace dominated one wall.

Kevin was friendly without being intrusive, smart enough to know when a man wants to be let alone, but attentive enough that everything was always taken care of. A nod or shake of the head when making eye contact was enough to refill a glass or be left alone for another ten minutes.

The hall leading to the kitchen and loo was just past the end of the bar, towards the back, and a small stage took up a corner opposite the front door and vestibule. A large picture window ran along most of the front wall beside the entrance, showing the rain-slicked streets reflecting the neon signs and yellowed solar streetlights beyond.

Hank favored this place, with its smells of decades of spilled alcohol, and often came here with friends. Silver had surveilled her, making sure she wasn't being followed or in any other danger from their activities in China. Just because Hank 'the Hawk' Smith constantly chattered through a 12,000-kilometer train trip, insisting on sticking with him, and being annoying in general, didn't mean he wanted her to come to harm.

Glancing in the mirror over the bar from his seat near the front window, Silver watched Hank and her friends laughing and drinking at a table near the empty stage. The half wall of the foyer and a coat rack blocked Hank's direct line of sight.

The dinner rush had come and gone, and the night crowd was settling in. Silver nursed his malt whiskey and the glass of water beside it.

The table with the group of twenty-somethings overflowed with laughter, and the next words caught Silver's ear.

"You had to run for your life from an angry mob in the Shaanxi province of China?" a man at Hank's table asked.

"I didn't run," Hank's lilting, light accent replied. "I crept away like a cat in an alley."

Silver lifted his eyes and glanced in the mirror, keeping his head bowed.

"I spent weeks finding the parts to build you the perfect weapon, set to your exacting standards; didn't you have it with you?" the man asked.

"Sydney's a fine girl," Hank giggled. "but she isn't suicidal and thought that discretion was the better part of valor. She, nor I, am an idiot."

"Okay, but tell us about this man," the woman at the table demanded, her voice thick with drink, "tall, dark, and handsome?"

"You're worse than him," Hank sighed and pointed across the table, "always thinking with your downstairs. But yes, he was tall."

"My downstairs?" the drunken friend slurred. "You can't even use the grown-up word for it?"

The group laughed.

"Slim, dark skin, half a meter taller than you or me Hank," the woman purred, leaning back in her chair, hands running down her sides before grasping the table in a white-knuckled grip. "And a shaved head? Mmm, mm, mm! I would take him down like a charging rhino, girl!"

Silver had heard enough and had no desire to have anything further to do with this woman, no matter how flattering a description and performance Hank's friend was giving the bar to witness.

Double tapping the cardphone sensor to pay, Silver nodded at Kevin, and slipped out the door. He had a long day tomorrow.

In the mirror behind the bar, Hank watched the tall, dark form slip out the door and her eyes narrowed. Raising her pint to her friends, she spoke.

"Here's to old friends," Hank toasted as the others raised their glasses, "and to the new."

Chapter 4

"China called, and it wants its dragon egg back," the large man behind the worn oak desk fiddled with the computer in front of him. Installed earlier in the week, it wasn't doing half of what his old computer had done. Typing on the flat sheet of graphene in front of him, he watched the image on the transparent graphene monitor switch scenes.

Sitting in one of the antique wood and black leather chairs—which were over a hundred years old, from the 1950s—Hank stared at the name placard on the desk. 'Dr. Howard Johns, Curator' was laser etched into the brass plate glued to the wood block. The office smelled of dust and old papers, and a thick layer of the former covered multiple stacks of the latter on every flat surface in the room. Books piled on shelves and tables, once neatly ordered, had folders and sheaves of papers heaped atop of them. Odd skulls, pottery, and artifacts sat on top of those, holding them down in case a window was opened.

"Mz. Smith?" Dr. Johns leaned forward, waving a hand through Hank's line of sight to get her attention, his corduroy coat whispering.

"Yes, Dr. Johns?" Hank looked up, smiling for a moment before her mouth twitched and settled into a grimace, lines wrinkling her forehead.

"You remind me of a basset hound I had," Dr. Johns tugged on his shaggy beard, his chair creaking under his weight as he leaned back, "she always thought she was in trouble, even when you waggled a treat at her."

"But, I should be in trouble. I was the one who recommended Joan." Her words rushed out, tumbling over one another, all in one breath. "I brought her on. Because of me, she has a priceless artifact that rightfully belongs to one of the most powerful governments in the world. And we left a dead British military officer in the shambles of one of the most important archeological sites in history."

Hank looked down again, fiddling with the buttons on her tan dungarees.

"Mz. Smith," Dr. Johns's lips tightened into a forced smile, which did nothing to set Hank's mind at ease, "you should stop reminding me of these facts. Stop telling on yourself. In fact, stop talking. Let me continue before I decide it's important to rehash all the things you put in your report, and then later told me in detail, and again repeated to me when you came into my office ten minutes ago. We have other pressing matters but can return to this item of business at a later time if you feel the need for further self-flagellation."

Hank glanced at him, nodded, and looked down at the name placard again.

"Very well then." Dr. Johns picked up the energy drink in front of him, drew deeply from it, and set it down with a thump.

Hank's eyes jumped to the spot, saw drops fly onto the surrounding documents, and cringed.

Before he could continue, someone knocked on the office door.

"Oh good," Dr. Johns sat upright, knitting his fingers together on the desk, "our first guest has arrived. Come in!"

The doorknob turned, and the door rattled. The squeak of wood on wood indicated that it had stuck to the frame again.

"You have to kick it," Dr. Johns shouted towards the door. "Give it a bit of a kick at the bottom and it'll open right up!"

The door thudded open. Silver, holding the knob, stopped it from slamming against the bookshelf.

He surveyed the room, pausing at the three floor-to-ceiling windows behind the desk. The center window showed a map of modern-day Iran, another image dating back to 1935—when it became Iran—and a third showing ancient Persia, pre-AD.

Silver glanced behind the door as he closed it.

As he crossed the room, his pressed black suit swished, his shiny grey tie and silver tie tack standing out against the black shirt.

"Welcome, Mr. Silver." Dr. Johns stood, leaned forward across the desk, and extended his hand in greeting.

"Thank you, Dr. Johns," Silver smiled, white teeth contrasting against his dark skin. "I'm glad you thought to request me for this job."

"Mz. Smith insisted." Dr. Johns looked pointedly at the younger woman.

Her mouth was agape at this comment. Her jaw snapped shut, and she gave a tight-lipped smile as she stood and turned to greet the newcomer.

"Silver," Hank pulled her shoulders back, her voice clipped, "good to see you again. Hope you made it off the train okay."

"Yes," Silver smiled at Hank, taking her hand in greeting, "I did fine, had some pressing matters to attend, so I had to leave suddenly. Hope it didn't offend that I wasn't able to say goodbye."

"Not at all. I'm used to the brusque and self-involved behavior of people from…" Hank tilted her head, her brow furrowing. "Where are you from, Silver? I don't recognize your accent. It's like Australian blended with Romanian."

"If you can't place my accent," Silver released her hand, moved to the windows, separated the Venetian blinds with two fingers, and looked out, "then you must not be used to my rude behavior."

"I never said rude." Hank shrugged and dropped back into her chair.

"Please," Dr. Johns interrupted, "I thought you two got along. Mz. Smith praised your competence and skills in her report."

"Appreciating one's abilities doesn't mean you like them." Silver turned from the window, moved past the desk, and traced a finger along the spines of the books on the shelves.

"Exactly," Hank nodded.

"I get that a lot." Silver stopped in the room's corner and turned back towards the desk, folding his hands behind his back. "Now, what can I do for you today, Dr. Johns?"

"The Emperor's Seal, maybe?" Hank muttered.

"Excuse me?" Dr. Johns' energy drink stopped centimeters from his mouth.

Silver glanced sideways at Hank; his face blank.

"Silver had the lost seal of Qin Shi Huang." Hank looked straight at a spot on the window frame behind Dr. Johns, her head held high and shoulders stiff. "He wouldn't ever answer me when I asked about it. I mentioned it in my report."

"Yes, well…" Dr. Johns set his drink down, liquid

sloshing in the can. Shuffling some papers to one side of his keyboard, he cleared his throat and looked at Silver. "Do you have this priceless historical artifact?"

"No, I don't." Silver paused for a moment, holding the curator's attention with his stare. "Feel free to search me if you have any doubt."

"Oh, I don't think that'll be necessary." Dr. Johns smiled and leaned back in his chair. "That's settled then!"

"Bills have to be paid somehow," Silver said, still staring at the curator.

"What was that?" Johns's eyes went wide as he sat upright again.

Hank's head snapped to look at the mercenary standing behind her.

A knock on the door drew the museum director's attention.

Silver glanced at Hank, who was staring at him, and gave her a wink.

Hank's forehead wrinkled and her mouth tightened.

"You have to kick it!" Dr. Johns yelled at the door. "In the bottom corner, just give it a good kick. It sticks!"

The door flew open, slamming into the bookshelf. Artifacts rocked from the impact and Hank leapt up. She rushed to steady them, catching a purplish-red orb that rolled off the shelf. Looking at it for a moment, she shook her head to clear it, and set the odd sphere back onto its silver, three-legged stand.

A tall man with stiff, short-cropped white hair strode into the room, his sharp white suit standing out against the dust, parchment, and wood grain that dominated the room.

"Welcome, Mr. Roberts," Dr. Johns stood, and leaning across his desk, extended his hand.

"Please," the man took the director's tanned hand into his own pale one, smiling, "call me Aaron."

Silver noted the sunburst tattoo peeking from beneath the man's starched cuff, as well as the tentacle visible above his collar.

"This is Mr. Silver and Mz. Hank Smith," Johns gestured towards each of the other two.

"Pleasure to meet you, Mr. Silver," Roberts said, taking Silver's hand. "Your reputation is impressive."

Hank stared at the contrast of the two men, then gave a little jerk, realizing Roberts had spoken to her.

"I'm sorry," Hank said, "I was, just that I, never mind. What was that?"

"Oh," Roberts smiled a crooked smile, tilting his head a bit and leaning towards Hank, "it's ok. Lots of women have that reaction to me, Ms. Smith. Or may I call you Hank?"

"It's Mz.," Hank stiffened and set her feet a shoulder-width apart.

"Pardon me?" Roberts continued to smile, stepping around the two chairs to get closer to Hank.

"Mz. Smith, not Ms.," Hank reached out her hand, and Roberts extended his to catch hers. Twisting her arm, she caught him by the elbow and spun him around to face the desk.

"Now please, Mr. Roberts," with a slight shove, she moved him towards the chairs, "have a seat so we may get on with business."

Roberts sat in a chair, looking back over his shoulder at Hank through slitted eyes.

Silver sat in the other chair, scooting it closer to the desk and bumping Roberts's chair.

"Ah," Silver said, patting the man's hand, "pardon me. I didn't mean to get you there."

Roberts's attention turned to Silver, who stared into the pale man's stark blue eyes with a small smile, eyebrows raised and head lowered slightly.

"Yes," Dr. Johns clapped his hands and rubbed them together, drawing everyone's attention to him, "shall we begin?"

Dr. Johns tapped at the flat keyboard on his desk and the windows' tinting darkened, leaving the maps on the middle window the centerpiece of attention.

"Aaron said he needed our professional help with a certain project," Dr. Johns began, leaning back in his chair, his energy drink in one hand and a laser pointer in the other.

"He also expressed that it has the potential for danger, and that's why we brought in Mr. Silver," Johns continued, pointing at Silver. A red dot appeared on Silver's black shirt; the light almost absorbed by the dark material.

Silver brushed at the spot, a crease appearing between his brows.

"Aaron, would you care to expand on what they'll be doing?" Johns raised the can in toast to the white-haired man.

"I'd be happy to." Roberts stood, brushing at his white suit.

Squeezing between the desk and Silver's knees— giving Silver the backside view, as opposed to the crotch view—Roberts slid past the mercenary to approach the maps.

"Thank you, Howard," Roberts nodded at the smiling curator, and pulled his left sleeve up, revealing his cardphone bracer. "You don't mind if I take over your presentation, do you?"

Fingers tapping at the display on his forearm, the maps on the window screen shifted, the oldest one of Persia becoming larger with details filling in.

"How did you get all of that information?" Dr. Johns gasped, "I haven't seen most of that before, and a lot of it is just historical theory!"

"I have resources your museum, or even your country does not," Roberts laughed, "the benefit of not being constrained by politics in the way a government is.

"And speaking of politics and history, I'll begin with a lesson in both," Roberts looked at Silver and smiled, "though I'm sure most of you know all this. Some of you are probably pretty ignorant."

Silver smiled back, raising an eyebrow.

"In 539 BC King Cyrus the Great ruled the Persian Empire," Roberts turned to the map, "under his rule, the world saw the birth of the greatest empire that ever existed up to that point.

"In the thirty years he ruled, he conquered the Median Empire, Lydian Empire, and Neo-Babylonian Empire," Roberts continued as Dr. Johns' red dot pointed out each area mentioned, "ruling from the Mediterranean Sea across Western Asia, and even into Central Asia."

"Showboat," Hank muttered under her breath.

"No, he wasn't," Roberts corrected her, his shoulders stiffening. With a wave of his hand, he caught the red dot and threw it aside.

Dr. Johns tapped on the side of his no longer functioning laser pointer, staring down its barrel.

"Didn't mean him," Hank muttered.

Silver snickered.

Dr. Johns hushed them. "Carry on, Aaron, please."

"Mr. Roberts, if you would please," Roberts glared at Dr. Johns, then turned back to the maps. "King Cyrus was the first ever to issue decrees on human rights. He freed slaves, declared all people had a right to choose their own religions, and even established racial equality.

"He did this for altruistic reasons, but also for business purposes." Roberts turned back to face the three. "Free people are always more productive and motivated than slaves and people living in fear."

"I really love history, Mr. Roberts," Hank said from where she stood in front of the bookshelves. "It's why I became an archeologist. But can you get to the part where you need my skills as an archeologist before another epoch passes and I'm inundated with work?"

"I understand, *Mz. Smith*," a snake-like smile spread across Roberts's face as he turned to Hank, "someone like you feels you have to prove yourself."

Hank stiffened, and Silver shifted in his chair, the lump under his armpit showing the outline of a gun.

"I'll get to the point," Roberts turned back to the map, a smile on his lips.

He held his hands up and pulled them apart. The map zoomed in, showing a golden oil lamp with a spout on one side and a handle on the opposite side, with the small notation next to it that said, 'artist rendition'.

"This is the Jazeer's Light, a simple, golden oil lamp," Roberts continued, "whose name translates to Victory's Light."

"Or Emphasis Light," Hank said from the back of the room, her arms folded across her chest.

"Excuse me?" Roberts turned, sighing, to look at the woman.

"If my ancient Persian holds up," Hank scoffed, moved around the chair Roberts vacated, and seated herself, "and it always does, Jazeer could mean victory or it could mean emphasis, as in it is the drive and purpose, rather than the end result."

Dr. Johns and Roberts both glared at Hank.

"I don't think Mr. Roberts is the type of man who's used to being interrupted, Hank," Silver said.

Roberts turned to him and nodded his thanks with a small smile and turned back to the screen.

"Perhaps you should save all helpful and useful information for after he's left," Silver added, as Roberts was about to continue.

The man spun about; his face contorted.

"Please, *Mr. Roberts,*" Silver leaned forward with a snake-like smile, "do go on, I need all the help I can get just to keep up."

"Rumor is," Roberts continued, his posture rigid, "this mythical symbol has resurfaced. Criminal families and organizations are fighting over it, hoping to become the one who possesses it and to unite all the crime syndicates—from the mafia to the yamaguchi-gumi—under one umbrella to become a world power in business, industry, and finance."

"And you want us to find it?" Silver asked.

Roberts nodded.

"And give it to you?" Silver asked.

Roberts nodded again.

"Why should we help you?" Silver leaned back, tugging his shirt cuffs out of his jacket sleeves.

"Mr. Silver," Roberts was cool, collected, and all business again now that he was back in his element, "for the same reason you do anything you do in your line of work: money. You do what I say, I pay you money.

"If you need more reasons," Roberts moved to put a hand on Johns's shoulder, "then consider the money we already give to the museum. How many archeological digs we sponsor, how many expeditions we fund, how many art shows we support, and so on. Also consider how it would be a shame if those suddenly could no longer happen because there wasn't enough money.

"Or if you need a bigger picture reason," Roberts let go of the curator's shoulder, leaned against the map behind him, and folded his arms across his chest, "the fighting amongst these criminal organizations are affecting trade and financial markets across the world.

"And if the crime families across the world become even more organized, they'd be able to challenge governments themselves, threatening the world economy with extortion and protection rackets on a global scale. We wouldn't want that, would we?

"This should appeal to every person in this room," Roberts's words slowed down, and he continued with a condescending tone. "Mz. Smith can research and follow the trail to the lamp. Mr. Silver makes sure she stays alive while she does that. You give it to me. I make the problem go away for good. And everyone wins. Is that simple enough for everyone here to understand?"

The trillionaire financier smiled, waiting for their answer.

Chapter 5

"Who gets the artifact when all of this is done?" Hank asked, scooting to the edge of her seat and leaning forward to put her elbow on the curator's desk.

"It would be safest with me," Roberts said, placing his fists on his hips and thrusting his chest out, "I have the money and power to keep it out of the hands of the peons that will come for it once we have it."

"I think it would be best in a museum," Hank's voice was tight and level.

"Maybe the museum should get it, but I don't think a museum would be able to keep it." Roberts scowled, shaking his head.

"What I think Mz. Smith is trying to say," Director Johns interrupted, his voice cracking, "is that, perhaps, after a brief respite, where the lamp is hidden away, for safety reasons, we could have it with us to document and classify it in a historical context."

Roberts turned to stare at the large man, who shrank back under his glare. Roberts's sudden smile made Johns flinch.

"Of course, Dr. Johns," Roberts spread his hands in front of him in surrender. "That makes perfect sense. Of course, the final decision will rest with the British Royal Museum's Board of Directors, as it should."

Silver looked around in the silence that followed, noting Johns's relief as the heavy-set man mopped at his brow with a handkerchief; Hank's frustration as she stared at the pale man in the white suit; and Roberts's smugness as he stood in front of the window, the light streaming from behind him giving him a halo and making his stiff, gelled hair sparkle.

"Well," Roberts broke the silence, smiling wide, "if everyone knows their job, then I'm satisfied to say that I'm done here."

The man brushed unseen flecks of dust from his pristine suit.

"Good work, people," Roberts clapped his hands and moved towards the door, "let's get this done."

The trillionaire walked to the open door, turned back to the room, winked and clicked his tongue while giving double finger guns to the three.

"Who's awesome?" Roberts asked, then spun on his heel and walked away, the click of his heels keeping time to the tune he whistled.

The three turned to look at one another, listening to the receding ticks of the man's hard-soled shoes.

"I don't think we should do this," Hank said.

"But Mz. Smith," Dr. Johns leaned forward, his hanky crushed in his massive fist, "this could mean a lot for the museum if you do it."

The big man froze, a look of realization crossing his features, then he dropped back into his chair.

"And it could mean even more if you don't," Johns mopped at his brow again.

"He would cut funding if you refuse," Silver said from behind Hank. "It's almost like extortion. Sounds like the methods any one of those mob groups that he's worried about stopping."

"You know what?" Hank spun in her seat to look at Silver. "I don't need your help. I'm quite capable of protecting myself. I can hit a moving target at a thousand meters with Sydney. After all, I saved your life, didn't I?"

"Yeah," Silver nodded, his voice low and slow as he stared at the floor in front of him, "you did. And because of that, I feel a bit obligated to repay that favor. And, it's been a while since I've run a job that means something more than a paycheck and doing this job might just be good for my soul. I need something more than black and white on occasion, and I think it's about time for my next dose. So, can you accept help, Hank, if it means helping someone else? And you might be good at a kilometer away, but I'm good at a meter away. We both have strengths, and they work well together."

"Look," Hank said, her voice sharp. She stopped and took a long look at Silver, her eyes softening.

She started again, this time with less bite in her voice. "Look, you're good at what you do, but you're driven by money. I've been screwed over by people who only pray to the money god, and don't have a higher reason for doing what they do. But remember, you can't…"

"I know how to do a job." Silver moved out of the corner, approaching Dr. Johns' desk as he spoke to Hank. "I've been doing this for two or three more decades than you."

Stopping in front of the large wood desk, Silver held his hand out to Dr. Johns, who stood and leaned across the desk to shake it with his own moist mitt.

"It was a pleasure to make your acquaintance, Mr. Silver." Johns sat back down, a large smile on his face. "I hope to see you again soon and have this artifact safely back in the right hands."

"I'll be ready to go within twenty-four hours," Silver strode towards the door, "barring any other obligations popping up, of course."

Silver pulled the door closed behind him as he left the room, tugging hard so it would close.

The two inside the room waited, listening for the receding footfalls, which never came.

"Barring any other obligations," staring at the door, Hank's voice rose in pitch and volume, imitating Silver. "Barring any other obligations? As if he has anything better to do. I've seen him, following me, lurking around, creeping on me. Why do we need him, anyway?"

"He comes highly recommended," Johns fiddled with his sheet of keyboard, waving it around and sending crumbs flying.

"What do you mean?" Hank turned to face her boss, standing and planting her fists on the desk. "I recommended him."

"Exactly what I mean," Johns said, tapping on his keyboard, shutting down the maps on the window screen.

Hank's mouth snapped shut. She stood up, removed her fists from the desk, and sighed.

"You believe in me that much?" Her voice sounded small in her own ears. "Even after the China fiasco."

"My dear," Johns stopped fidgeting and looked Hank straight in the eye, "I've always believed in 'the Hawk', since the day you bounced through the door, a first year college intern, talking about how you're going to make a difference in this world and make your family proud. You have a fine eye for the work, and so much more. The eyes of a hawk, but in so many more ways than others would think or give you credit for.

"And the China fiasco, as you so deftly dubbed it,"

Johns waved his hands in the air as if clearing an unpleasant smell, "only made me have more confidence in you, not less. You took a difficult situation and came out alive, but also with a new resource. And you didn't try to pass the blame to anyone or anything else. You stood up and took full responsibility."

"And that makes me trustworthy, eh?" Hank smiled.

"It makes you trustworthy, yes," Johns looked back down, picking up his laser pointer and poking at it, "but also a bit stupid. You really should learn to let things go and stop worrying so much about what other people think."

Johns smacked the device with two fingers.

"Damn that man," the director muttered. "I think Roberts broke my favorite pointer."

"I just don't know if I should take this job, Croaker." Silver approached a knot of people, quieting and stepping to one side to avoid going through the middle of them, his eyes moving from person to person.

"Look," the gruff voice said into his ear after a moment, "you need to work or you'll go stir crazy. We both know that. You're the kind of man that always must be doing something, otherwise you're gonna create trouble for yourself, and in turn, all the people around you. And that includes me. I don't want to have to deal with that kind of crap, so you're going to take this job."

"You're not wrong," Silver glanced at the

cardphone on his wrist, checking the incoming text that beeped into his ear over Croaker's voice, "but I don't know if bringing Hank into this sort of thing is the right thing to do."

"This girl, the 'Hawk' as she's called, can take care of herself. You're just there as extra insurance. But whine to somebody who cares," Croaker muttered, "I'm your agent, not your friend. I'm not here to hug you and tell you that it'll all be okay. I don't watch rom-coms, pass the tissues, and share a tub of ice cream with you."

"Nobody says rom-coms anymore, Croaker." Silver stopped and looked around, checking the street signs, then pulling up the maps on the cardphone.

"Whatever," papers rustled through the earpiece, a sign that Croaker was about to make an excuse to get off the phone, "why don't you go find someone who cares, or at least you pay to talk to? Make a new friend, get a dog, go to a therapy website, but stop bugging me with all this needy crap."

"Yeah," Silver moved down the street with a purposeful stride, "I'm already on it. And why don't you move into the twenty-first century and stop writing everything down on paper?"

"Yeah," Croaker's voice was distant, and Silver knew the man was using a hand-held again, "that ain't gonna happen. I wasn't born in this millennium, and I don't feel the need to conform to technology that's just going to fail soon enough. You fit in better with that stuff."

"Funny how that worked out, isn't it?" Silver heard Croaker's non-committal grunt. "You were the inventor, tinkerer, and gadgetphile, and here you are avoiding everything with technology. And I was a boots-on-the-ground grunt, and I'm soaking up as much of it as I can."

"You were anything but a grunt," Croaker's voice was loud again, but muffled and scratchy from the sound of his stubble on the mic as he held the phone between his shoulder and cheek.

The line went dead at the vague compliment.

Silver chuckled, used to how Croaker ended calls.

Leaving the museum district, Silver navigated through the crowds towards The Cask & Custard Pot and arrived less than a half hour later.

Entering the dim interior, Silver headed towards the same spot he'd sat the night before.

One man sat at the other end of the bar and a table had a man and a woman at it. All three glanced towards the door when Silver came in.

Kevin emerged from the kitchen as Silver settled onto the bar stool and pulled a coaster in front of him.

"You alright, mate?" Kevin asked, setting the rack of glasses he was carrying on the sink behind the counter.

"Doing okay," Silver said.

"You looking for a meal or libations, then?" Kevin stood a head taller than most men, and Silver looked up to meet his eyes.

"Just a water and two fingers of whiskey." Silver glanced towards the waitress carrying three plates to the table with the couple.

"Coming right up." Kevin turned and reached for a green bottle on the glass shelf in front of the mirror on the back wall. "Probably not my business, but it doesn't seem like someone is alright when they pop in before lunch and order whiskey without food."

Silver shrugged.

"Well, I'll leave you to it then," Kevin set down the whiskey—which had a spot more than two fingers—and a glass of water, "but remember, bartenders listen for less than a therapist, and we don't need to know your last name. You can always talk to a friend or your family. Let me know if I can be of any further help."

"Not much chance of me talking to friends or family," Silver sipped at the whiskey, "don't have many friends. Any friends, really."

"And what about family?" Kevin turned back towards Silver, leaning his elbow on the bar.

"They're," Silver paused, "estranged, and very far away from here. I haven't seen them in a long time and won't be able to see them again…for a very, very long time."

"Then it sounds like you're in a bit of a quandary, doesn't it?"

"Actually, Kevin," Silver pushed a straw into the water, capped it with his finger, and then lifted it and moved it over the whiskey to let a few drops escape into the amber liquid, "maybe I could use an outside opinion."

Kevin nodded, pulled a glass from the rack, dried it with a towel, and set it on a shelf.

"I may be putting someone in danger." Silver paused and took a drink from the whiskey, holding it in his mouth for a moment before swallowing. "And I'm not sure if that's the right thing to do."

"So," Kevin kept working, not looking towards Silver, "you're going to push them into traffic or something, then?"

"No, nothing like that." Pausing for a moment, Silver considered. "Actually, a lot like that. I took a job as a bodyguard, and it'll be dangerous. And the person I'm supposed to guard may not be up to the task."

"So, kidnapping then?" Kevin dried another glass.

"No, what's that have to do with anything?"

"Are you forcing them into this?" Kevin poured a lager from the tap into the pint glass he'd cleaned. Lifting it, he tilted it towards Silver, "No man should drink alone. Cheers, mate."

The two men clinked glasses, and Kevin took a pull. Smacking his lips, he asked, "Coercing them, pushing them, tricking them?"

"No," Silver said, "I see what you're doing. No, they're perfectly aware that there'll probably be danger. But I'm not sure they're ready for it."

"Sounds like the decision isn't yours to make," Kevin swiped a finger up the side of the glass to stop an errant drip, "but maybe you want to keep them safe because you're a good man, and maybe even care about this person enough to give a damn if they live or die. Not that whatever you're doing could lead to death."

Silver stared into his whiskey glass, considering the man's words.

Kevin watched him for a moment, then left him to his own thoughts.

"Are you home, Darcy?" Hank shouted.

She closed the apartment door behind her, tossed her keycard on the table beside the door, and scooped up Frick who'd been rubbing against her legs.

"Yeah," Darcy called back, "I'm in the bathroom, getting ready for work. Do you need in here?"

"No, thanks." Hank moved through the kitchen,

stopping to pet Frack and received a glare in return, and then to her bedroom. "I'm only here to pack up. I'm going on another adventure!"

"Oh, how exciting!" Darcy's voice echoed. "Where to this time?"

"Not sure." Hank pulled down her soft-sided suitcase, which also had backpack straps. It didn't hold much, but it'd be enough. "And I've an escort this time."

"Didn't you have Joan last time?" Darcy's voice came from the living room.

"Yeah," Hank threw one dress outfit into the bag, then moved to what she called her 'adventure gear,' which consisted of lots of beige things with lots of pockets, "but this time, it's Silver."

"The guy from the train in China?" Darcy's voice was muffled, and Hank could hear her rummaging through the refrigerator.

"Yeah," Hank held up two sidearms, trying to decide which one to pack, "but this guy and I seem to have a connection, an understanding, a real, um, thing instead of whatever it was that Joan and I had."

"So, you don't think this guy will try to kill you?" Darcy's voice was muffled by chewing this time.

"No." Hank shrugged and threw one weapon into her bag and tucked the other into her hygiene kit. "I saved his life, so I figure he owes me one and is less likely to try to bump me off because of that."

"That's good to hear," Darcy's voice came from her bedroom.

"Dr. Johns said I should stop worrying about what other people think; what do you think about that?" Hank lifted Frick out of her suitcase and set him on the floor, moving to her computer to load info onto her cardphone.

"I think you missed the point if you have to ask me what I think about it," Darcy's voice came from just outside the room.

"You're probably right," Hank sighed. "I just like talking to folks and learning what they think and why."

"There's a difference between wanting to know what folks think, and needing to know they think you're doing okay," Darcy's voice drew further away, and Hank heard the front door open. "I'm off now, kisses sweetie!"

"Have fun storming the castle," Hank shouted back, "and take care of Frick and Frack while I'm gone!"

The sound of the front door closing ended the conversation.

Silver stepped out of the Uber Fleet car onto the sidewalk. The taxi hummed away, dodging into traffic to find the next call.

Beeps, buzzes, whistles, or customized driving tones issued from cars zipping past, alerting pedestrians of their presence; something that was necessary since the internal combustion engines had almost totally disappeared. There'd been an upsurge in people being hit by the electric cars because they didn't make enough noise, so the automobile industry came up with ways to alert less-aware people, such as people who couldn't bother looking up from their phones.

There were also fewer private cars now, having become more of a luxury than most could afford. The past few decades had seen the expansion of the infrastructure; car-sharing, ridesharing, new bus lines, train lines, and even newer concepts on the rise.

Silver looked around at elevated train supports being built to allow more foot and electric bicycle traffic on the ground, while mass transit whizzed past overhead.

Pedestrians had the sidewalks. The lane closest to that was for individual wheeled transportation—such as bikes, skates, skateboards, and so on—and the center lane for private vehicles and delivery vehicles. The overhead tracks would also provide some cover for the people below when it was raining, like now.

The pungent, sharp smell of ozone—rather like chlorine—permeated the air. It was the mix of that clean smell after a rain, and the result of hundreds of electric vehicles. Doomsayers were already predicting the catastrophic long-term results of a buildup of the ozone layer from electric vehicles, forgetting about the events just a few decades before with the carbon emissions buildup, and the hole in the ozone layer a few decades before that.

Silver slid through the thick lunch crowd, moving back to work or to their preferred restaurant. Zippy Burger had a line along the sidewalk—which Silver had to push his way through—waiting for their various vegan and poultry sandwiches that were all flash sear-cooked. They wrapped all items in seasoned rice paper, so there was no waste, and they only offered drinks to people who brought their own refillable container. The franchise chain was a result of the beef ban of the twenties, where a panicky public pushed for the limiting of beef production because of health and obesity issues, as well as how beef production contributed to the green-house gas effect.

Turning down a side alley, the dark-skinned mercenary made his way towards his private warehouse. Moving past dumpsters and recycling deposit bins, he glanced up to see the older woman he paid to watch his place—her brightly colored outfit drawing his eye—give him a nod and thumbs up from her third-floor fire escape window.

Another block down, Silver paused next to a man hunched under a blue tarp spread between a dumpster, pinned under its lid, and a small crate on the ground, creating a makeshift lean-to.

The man wore a green flannel shirt over a dingy white t-shirt, and a half-unzipped maroon hoodie over it all. He pulled a small chunk of bread from the crusty loaf in his hand and popped it into his mouth, staring up at Silver through blood-shot eyes.

"Got anything?" Silver didn't look at the man with the patchy beard, instead watching the door of his warehouse another block away.

"Three people, boss," the man said, tossing breadcrumbs to a rat a few feet away. "One Asian kid watched your place for an hour or two before I chased him away. The other two were Mormons, or Jehovah's Witnesses, or some such group. White shirts, black ties, name badges. Kinda men-in-black sorts, maybe."

"What kind of Asian was the kid?" Silver scanned the rooftops.

"What does that mean?" The man scratched at his beard and squinted up at Silver.

"Indian, Japanese, Korean, Russian?" Silver paused and sighed. "They're all from the Asian continent. It's offensive to lump them altogether, stop living in the teens and come forward to today."

"Whatever boss," the man looked back down, "he

was Japanese or Chinese, one of those with slanted eyes."

"You're a moron," Silver dug in his pocket, "but you're useful."

"Thanks," the man cackled, "hard to get you riled up. It's fun."

Silver dropped a pack of plastic cards in a rubber band in the man's lap.

"That gang won't bother you again," he gestured at the cards, "those are their pre-purchase cards. They'll get you some food, clothes, and maybe a bottle. I included a Zippy Burger card for your extra effort. I appreciate it."

"Thanks again, boss." The man palmed the stack of cards, dropping them into an inner coat pocket.

Silver took a step towards his warehouse.

"Oh," he paused, turning back to the man on the ground, "what happened to the God peddlers?"

"They're still inside," the man coughed into his elbow, "she used some code card to bust your security on the door while he looked around and then went right in like they lived there."

Silver stared at the man, who was now bouncing a small red ball on the asphalt in front of him.

"I take back the useful thing, and double down on the moron thing," Silver growled. "You'd better move along while I go greet my guests. You don't want to get caught in the after party."

"Yeah, ok boss." The man collected his few things, crawled out of the makeshift shelter, and stood and limped away.

Silver watched him until he turned the corner at the end of the alley.

Reaching under his coat, Silver drew out his

firearm and moved towards his front door and the unwelcome guests, checking his cameras through his phone. Once he'd determined where his guests were, he knew what he had to do. After swiping his cardphone along the sensor to open the door, he burst into his safe house.

Travis I. Sivart

Chapter 6

Silver rolled to the right and behind the metal cabinet storing tools and ballistic armor materials. He came up in a crouch and peeked around the edge of the cabinet.

In the middle of the warehouse Silver used as a combat training room and vehicle workshop sat a man and a woman with raven hair on the threadbare couch. Two equally threadbare mid-century barrel chairs were on each side of the couch.

A series of two-story, double-pole support beams every six meters ran the thirty-meter length of the area. His apartment—at the far side of the space and up a narrow flight of stairs—looked undisturbed, as did the workout room underneath it.

To the left of the door were Silver's vehicles: a sleek black sports car, a motorcycle, and an experimental vehicle that worked with an electromagnetic power source and guidance system.

Neatly organized, low shelves of weapons, gear, and other items filled the space between the sitting area and the apartment, across from the vehicles. A desk with a state-of-the-art computer was by the wall, facing into the warehouse.

Both intruders wore pressed black suits with white shirts that contrasted with their olive skin. Black name tags with white lettering showed on their breast pockets.

The uninvited visitors stared at Silver over the top of magazines held in their hands.

"Really, Mr. Silver," the man folded his magazine and laid it across his lap, "there's no need for that."

"What do you want?" Silver looked at the security panel on the wall, checking how many people were inside the building. Only the three of them registered to the sensors, confirming what his phone—and his lookout—had told him.

"Just to talk," the woman said without looking up from the magazine she was reading.

"About what?" Silver keyed a code into his cardphone, activating a secondary security system.

The system kicked in and Silver flooded with confidence. In seconds, the cameras would begin recording, identifying his adversaries, feeding him info, as well as trigger the subdual protocols in place.

"You seek the Jazeer's Light," the woman said, looking up from her periodical, tilting her head as if listening to a distant noise. Keying something into the cardphone on her own wrist, Silver's wall display went dead.

"Why should that matter to you?" Silver growled as the display winked out, and began punching at his cardphone, trying to get it back online.

"We have parties who'd rather you didn't." The man stood and dusted off his black slacks.

"What if I don't care?" Silver gave up on the technology and braced himself for a more direct interaction.

"Then it may mean your life." The woman tossed her magazine onto the couch, stood, and drew two short black rods from her jacket.

"Or yours," Silver growled and stood, drawing firearms from a shoulder holster and an ankle holster, leveling them at the intruders.

The woman pressed a button on the metal tubes. They quadrupled in length, arcs of electricity rippling along them.

Silver squeezed his triggers in rapid succession, aiming one at the man and the other at the woman, firing in controlled bursts.

The man dove behind the couch, and the woman swung her batons in an arc. The electrical hum became more frenetic, and a burst of blue energy lit the room as the rods drew the bullets to them, striking them.

"Neat trick, lady," Silver aimed both weapons at the woman, "but can they block double the bullets?"

Silver opened fire.

The woman crouched, making herself a smaller target, her batons weaving in a figure eight. Bullets sparked against the electromagnetic barrier that burst into existence in front of her.

Silver dropped back behind the counter to reload. Hitting the magazine release with his thumbs, he popped the used ones out and snapped new ones into place from his belt.

Silver stood up, and a fist connected with his face. The man stood in front of him, swinging again.

Silver threw his forearm up to block it, moving the second firearm into play underneath the man's limb to shoot into the man's belly. The man flew back, the hole in his shirt revealing the bulletproof graphene vest underneath.

The woman leapt across the coffee table, charging the mercenary. The metal poles in her hands connected with Silver's shoulders, electricity traveling down his arms. His hands went numb, and one gun clattered to the floor and the other to the counter. Silver reached for the weapon on the counter, and the woman swept it away with her electro-rod.

Silver darted to his left, towards the tool pit near his vehicles, but the man lifted one of the barrel chairs and threw it in his path. Silver's legs tangled in the furniture, and he stumbled into a metal support pole, falling to the ground.

Pushing off the pole and tumbling, heels-over-head, Silver rolled backwards and sprung to his feet. Reaching behind him—keeping his eyes on his opponents—he grabbed the first thing he found.

Pulling a handheld, portable propane welding torch from behind him, the three glanced at it, then looked back at each other. With a shrug, Silver clicked the auto-start button, and the blue flame burst to life with a noise like angry static.

Crouching to lower his center of gravity—torch in his right hand and his left hand held out to the side, ready to block a strike or score an extra hit—Silver circled to the left, trying to get closer to his weapons cache.

The woman ran her electro-rods along one another, creating a shower of sparks that burst with brilliant blue light.

Silver averted his eyes for a moment.

That was all the woman's partner needed, and he lunged for Silver. Grabbing him, the attacker wrapped his arms around Silver's midsection and pinned the man's arms against his sides. They tumbled to the ground.

Silver jerked the propane torch upward, touching the man's elbow with the blue blaze. The intruder's jacket sleeve burst into flame and the smell of burning flesh flooded the air.

Screaming, the man tightened his grip, refusing to

let go.

The torch continued up the man's bicep, and forced him to release Silver with that arm, his muscles and sinew melting under the intense heat.

Silver, the torch free, moved the flame towards the man's face.

The screaming intensified, and the man's tenuous grip with his remaining arm loosened. Silver broke free of the hold, pushed to his feet, and kicked out. The foot connected with the man's bubbling face and skin melted away. The man fell back.

The woman moved forward, electro-rods swishing in a crisscross pattern.

Silver stumbled backwards, leaning away from the attack, driven further from the weapons cache.

Thrusting the torch forward to push the woman back, Silver watched her take the bait and swing her right electro-rod in to strike his hand holding the torch.

His left hand shot out, grabbing her wrist and twisting it. The sound of bones snapping made Silver wince.

The woman dropped her weapon and the electrical charge faded from it as it hit the floor.

Silver twisted the wrist further.

The man on the floor kicked the back of Silver's knee, taking his leg out from underneath him. The woman's remaining electrified baton grazed Silver's shaved head and his vision lit up with starbursts of light and pain.

Moments later, Silver's awareness returned. He could hear the propane torch clanking as it spun away, skittering along the floor. The male intruder lay beside him, still clutching his face and twitching, soft whimpers coming from him.

The woman stood over Silver, straddling his prone form, thrusting her remaining baton into Silver's gut, causing him to scream in pain and writhe underneath her.

He blacked out again.

Returning to awareness for the second time since this encounter began, Silver realized his hands had been zip-tied in front of him. The woman still stood over him. The man beside him had quieted and lay motionless, and the distant sound of the propane torch sputtered then regained strength. He heard the faint sound of fire crackling, and smelled burned hair, flesh, and wood in the air.

"We just wanted to talk," the woman was calm, her face neutral, though she was panting with exertion, "we did not want it to come to this."

"You have a funny way of showing it." Silver moved his feet, checking if they were bound as well. They weren't.

"You drew weapons," the woman waved her baton to emphasize her words, "you fired upon us."

"And why are you dressed like Mormons, or Latter-Day Saints, or whatever? Is the church interested in this thing, too?"

"Zoroaster says to have wisdom in all your actions, to renew the world, not destroy it as the western cultures glorify."

"What do you want?" Silver flexed his wrists and felt the zip strips bite into his flesh.

"We want you to stop seeking the Light of Jazeer," the woman straightened, unaware of her body language as she began what felt like scripted lines to Silver, "we want you to leave it alone."

"Why?" Silver's eyes narrowed. "Who sent you to

stop me?"

Across the warehouse, the sound of the fire flared, popping, and the woman turned to look.

"I think there is danger here," the woman said.

Silver, taking advantage of her distraction, twisted his body, pulled his legs up, and thrust his feet into her midsection. She flew backwards, dropping her weapon.

The baton came down onto Silver's belly before the electricity died out, and his body tightened in a spasm.

The metallic rod spun to one side, and Silver rolled to his belly, pushed up with his hands and stood on shaking legs.

"We need to leave. Your weapons are going to explode!" The woman was looking over her shoulder towards the shelves of gear and ammunition across the warehouse. Turning back to look at her fallen partner, fear on her face, she moved towards the man. "We must get out of here. Help me get him out of here! Kazemi must know you will stop this foolish errand!"

The dark-haired woman rushed to her fallen partner, grabbing his arms and trying to turn his body to drag him to the door, which still stood ajar.

"Kazemi?" Silver hesitated as he moved towards the door. "Is that a person's name, an organization, or something else?"

A series of small explosions began in the center of the warehouse. Glancing that way, Silver could see crates of cigars burning below the metal containers that held his stock of grenades and ammo.

"Help me," the woman struggled to pull her partner to safety.

"The name, what does it mean?" Silver moved towards the woman.

"Saman Kazemi," the woman dragged the unconscious man, pulling him with one hand, the other hand flopping to one side, showing the wrist was broken, "he's a man."

Silver rushed forward to help her.

An explosion shook the building, throwing them backwards. Silver slammed against the door.

Coughing, he looked around. Sparks danced in a dense black cloud. He couldn't see the woman through the smoke-filled air.

Pulling at the door with his bound hands, Silver stumbled outside and was thrown to the ground as a series of smaller explosions went off.

Rolling over, Silver saw the roof of the building burst outward.

Covering his head with his arms, pieces of metal showered down around him.

When the manmade rain of fire slowed, Silver stood and took stock of his surroundings.

The warehouse was in flames, onlookers already gathering in the street to gawk and stare.

Reaching into a pocket with one hand, the other hand still bound to the first, he pulled out a pocketknife. Unfolding the blade, he flipped it around and inserted it between his wrists and sawed at his bonds.

The plastic snapped and blood rushed back into his hands.

Rubbing at his wrists, he looked up and down the street; people were watching him.

He glanced up at the building and walked sideways into the crowd to blend in.

"Are you ok?" an older woman dressed in garish colors asked him.

It was the woman he paid to watch his property from her third-floor window.

He nodded.

"I was walking by and it just exploded," Silver shouted loud enough for nearby people to hear, pulling his jacket sleeves over his wrists to cover the ligature marks.

People began muttering, each telling a similar story to anyone who would listen.

"Think you can help me out with a distraction?" Silver said softly, leaning towards his informant.

After a quick nod from the woman, Silver moved away from her.

The older lady began wailing and shouting about her cat missing, drawing the forming crowd's attention as Silver slipped away.

"Agatha," Silver said, lifting his wrist to speak into his cardphone on its bracer, "locate Hank Smith."

"Yes, sir," a mature and mildly feminine voice said from the cardphone, "searching her location now. Accessing street cams and social media feeds."

"Also, check news feeds for any violence in the past two hours within London, especially with mention of anyone fitting Hank's description."

"Yes sir," Agatha replied, her voice gentle but professional. "Mz. Smith located, and directions loaded to your interface. Will you also need directions to one of your safe houses for resupply?"

"Only if it's on the way to Hank." Silver checked the display and turned east, heading in the direction indicated.

Travis I. Sivart

Chapter 7

Silver stood under the canopy in front of a Chinese restaurant, watching the bookstore across the street. The rain had set in and the smell in the air had that odd blend of wet asphalt, ozone from the electric cars, and the dingy dank of the city.

Neon signs blinked in the grey haze, clearer in the puddles than when looking at them directly. A bit of jazz music came from a second-story club nearby, the high-hat and standup bass echoing off the close-set buildings.

People pressed past him, their heads down in the weather as they attempted to stay dry by holding various personal items above their heads, popping their coat collar up and dodging from awning to awning, or even using old-fashioned umbrellas.

Silver had stopped by a safe house; and though it was little more than a large closet with access through metal cellar doors from an alley, it was enough to replace his singed outfit and gather a few extra pieces of gear.

He pulled a stringy pile of noodles from the folded wax paper carton, leaned against the brick and stucco wall, and slurped them down.

His phone beeped.

Are you stalking me? A message from Hank read, *I can see you over there, you're not even trying to be discreet. I mean, really? I'm at my book club, and we're discussing a very interesting fictional biography about Indiana Jones. Why are you here?*

I had an incident today, Silver typed, avoiding using voice to text where he could be overheard, *and decided that being a visual deterrent is the best way to make sure you're safe.*

You're not a deterrent, you're a target.

Tomato, tomato. Silver typed, glancing up and down the street, then finished his message before hitting send. *Besides, I have a plan.*

Why would you even worry about me? The reply appeared in real time, backspacing to correct an error, *I can take care of myself.*

So can MMA superstars, Silver snorted as he typed, *but they still have bodyguards. You're my meal ticket, and I'd rather not miss a meal because I didn't do my job.*

I can see that. A photo of Silver accompanied the reply, two red circles on it highlighting a noodle hanging from his mouth, and another stray noodle curled on his well-polished shoe.

Before he could construct a reply, a laughing cat cartoon popped onto his cardphone, then another, and another, until his whole screen—including the keyboard—was covered with giggling felines.

The door to the bookstore opened, accompanied by the tinny, jangling sound of the brass bells hanging down. Hank strode out, pausing for a moment to look up and down the street, then glanced upward and scanned the buildings. She took in the whole scene without more than a moment passing.

Hank crossed the road, dancing around the neon-shimmering puddles, and stopped beside Silver. She leaned over to look at the dozens of amused kittens on his device.

With a snicker, Hank reached over and poked the

screen a few times, and they disappeared.

"I hacked you," Hank giggled, "with kitties."

"Yeah, kid," Silver grumbled, "good work. That'll be just what we need to find this thing and get it from whoever has it."

"So why are you here?" Hank looked up at Silver. "I know you said because you had something happen, but why not call me? Or just come inside?"

Silver shrugged.

Hank paused for a moment, then stepped back a pace, folded her arms, and rested her chin on a fist, inspecting Silver.

"You weren't the bait," she smirked. "I was. You were here, in plain sight, taunting whoever it is that you had this 'incident' with, using me to draw them out."

"Don't worry about it," Silver said, clicking his phone back into its wrist socket. "I wasn't putting you in any danger."

"Yes, you were," Hank's smirk grew into a smile, "but that means you know I can handle myself, and that's why you didn't feel the need to warn me ahead of time."

"Sure, kid," Silver shook the stray noodle off his shoe, "let's go with that."

"But you made yourself quite obvious to me and whoever else this is," Hank went on, her thumb stroking her chin in an absent gesture, "meaning you wanted to be seen by both of us. Why? I mean, if you're going to use me as bait, you should hide. Unless you wanted to be seen, but then the question is; who did you want to see you? Them or me?"

"Okay, kid," Silver turned and tossed his empty food container into a rubbish bin embedded in the side of a building, "I think we need to focus more on where these people are than my motives."

"You know," Hank left her hand on her chin, but moved the other to her hip, which now jutted out to one side in a rebellious manner, "the 'kid' thing isn't going to work for me. Though I may not have your decades of experience and body aches, I'm a very capable adult, not some child. You can call me Hank, Hawk, Smith, Mz. Smith, Charlie the Unicorn, or Zaphod Beeblebrox, but not kid, sport, tiger, champ, princess, baby, darling, sweat pea, honey, or giggly cute face snuggle bug. Though I will accept buddy, pal, chum, mate, or partner on occasion."

Silver's forehead wrinkled as he turned his full attention to the woman beside him. She was no longer looking at him, instead she had turned away and was looking upward towards the skyline, one hand still planted on her hip, and the other back on her chin. She didn't look mad, instead, she appeared amused.

"Fair enough." His frown lines disappeared, and he smiled. "I don't like being called princess either, but the others don't bother me."

As Silver watched, Hank's face changed to a more serious and focused look.

"What is it, Beeblebrox?" Silver paused. "Wait a second, isn't that the two-headed guy from…"

"The number of heads doesn't matter," Hank interrupted, "it's the two brains, one very smart and cunning, the other silly and unpredictable. It's a nickname that dates back to right before I picked up my first firearm and got the nickname 'the Hawk'.

"But that isn't important right now," Hank snapped her head back to Silver, her arms dropping to her sides, "you want to know where they are? The people looking for us?"

Silver nodded, looking up and down the street.

"Nope," Hank's voice had become serious and monotone, "two on the third-floor fire escape, one building to the left of the bookstore; two on the rooftop of the building we're in front of; two in the mouth of the alley a block down, across the street; and four just came around the corner to your left, my right. And I also noticed, they're all Oriental, as in they're most likely from Japan, China, Korea, or surrounding areas. Hard to tell in the dim light and rain."

"You got skills, ki..." Silver swallowed the word, "...partner. I think we should lead them on a merry chase and get them..."

He was cut off when Hank spun into action, tossing a handful of small children's jacks towards the approaching four that were closest. Pulling out her phone, she activated an app, snapped a picture of the four, and punched something into the interface.

"Cover your eyes," Hank muttered.

"What are you doing, ki..." Silver never finished his sentence.

A series of blinding flashes lit the street, huge shadows climbing the sides of the buildings.

Passerbys threw their arms up, covering their eyes as the four approaching people did the same.

Hank grabbed Silver's wrist, as he rubbed at his eyes, and pulled him into the Chinese restaurant he'd been loitering in front of. He stumbled after.

"What do you know about your attackers from the incident?" Hank shouted, dragging Silver around the counter, dodging the surprised employees of the eatery.

"They mentioned Zoroaster." Silver pulled his wrist from Hank's grasp and followed her. "They had an accent; I'm guessing from the Middle East."

She led him through the galley-style kitchen, towards the back door, which was open to an alley except for a screen door and an air curtain, a powerful overhead fan unit blowing straight down to keep any insects from entering.

They pushed through the screen door and into the alley. The back street was wide enough for two cars to pass one another or a single trash truck to move down. Reusable wooden vegetable crates, plastic milk crates, and CO_2 canisters were stacked outside the restaurant's back door. A sour smell hung in the air despite the steady drizzle, and a trickle of oily rainwater ran a jagged path around dumpsters, loose trash, and the few irritated residents of the alley that included rats and people alike.

"Disciples of Zarathustra?" Hank looked up and down the alley, up to the rooftops, and then said over her shoulder. "It's an old monotheistic religion, based on truth."

"Does that matter?" Bursts of light still danced in Silver's vision, though it was clearing.

"Indeed, it can tell us a lot about the people chasing us." Hank moved to the right, deeper into the dark alley, lit only by dim fluorescent bulbs over the doors leading to a variety of businesses.

"This way." She picked up the pace to a careful jog. "The basic beliefs are Humata, Hukhta, Huvarshta; which means good thoughts, good words, and good deeds. Not a bad philosophy to live by."

Silver grunted an acknowledgement as he trailed behind her and blinked a series of blinks that activated the low-light vision feature of his digital contact lenses. It also soothed the ache from the flashes that had blinded him less than a minute before.

"They feel that there is only one path, the path of Truth." Hank weaved around a plastic-covered box where a pair of denim-covered legs stuck out and they could hear a gentle snore. "They do the right thing because it's the right thing to do, and feel that rewards will come to them from those actions."

"That seems a bit overly optimistic," Silver said as they turned right at a t-intersection. He heard the screen door—behind him and around the corner—hit the wall as it slammed open and closed. Shouting voices in a language he didn't know echoed off the stone valley of the surrounding buildings.

"Well," Hank fell silent to sprint down a semi-clear straightaway, trying to reach the next turn before their pursuers were close enough to follow.

They slowed as they came to two cars parked in the alley beside one another and turned sideways to squeeze between them.

Hank continued.

"They think that the purpose of life is to 'be among those who renew the world, to make the world progress towards perfection'," she interspersed her words between pants, coming out from between the cars and picking up a steady jog again.

"I have to admit," Silver said between breaths and long-legged strides, stopping himself from going his full speed to avoid leaving Hank behind, "the two who were waiting for me in my place didn't try to ambush me, and were trying to talk instead of fight. I..."

Silver paused as they leaped a pile of trash spilling out into the alley from an overflowing dumpster. He noticed Hank was keeping up, and though they were both breathing heavily from the workout, neither lagged behind.

Hank looked at him, waiting for him to continue.

They burst into a busy street. Foot traffic was thick, and cars zipped past. Hank led the way, pushing past people and into the street.

The two moved forward into the traffic, dodging cars only to stop suddenly on the white lines between lanes, then leaping forward to get to the sidewalk on the other side of the street.

Cars honked as the gang following them burst into the road, slamming their hands on hoods of cars and shouting at drivers.

Hank and Silver darted down another alley.

"Go on," Hank urged as they cleared the obstacle and picked up speed again.

Silver didn't say anything for a few moments.

"They didn't want to fight." Silver fell a few steps behind his companion, knocking over a couple of trash cans to create another obstacle. "They wanted talk. And instead, they died."

"Did you see their corpses?" Hank asked over her shoulder.

"What?" Silver considered the question when she didn't respond. "No, I didn't."

"Then you can't be sure they're dead, can you?" She panted with a sardonic tone.

"No," he agreed, moving faster in another straightaway, "but if they did die, why would they have been willing to?"

"They have a fravashi, we all do," Hank continued, moving through the maze of small alleys that held a series of clothing lines above, "a guardian angel or spirit, that watches over their soul, which they call the urvan, which has been around since Mazda created all of existence."

"I'm not sure how that explains anything," Silver said, taking a sharp corner, and bouncing off the close wall.

"The fravashi gathers their experience and knowledge the fourth day after death, using it to help in the continuing battle between truth and falsehood on a cosmic level." Hank slowed to look at Silver. "Life is temporary, but the things they do in that life helps in the long run."

Shouts from behind warned them that their enemies were closing on them.

Silver drew the two short silver blades concealed under the back of his jacket, locked into a harness, and threw a glance behind them, looking for the pursuers.

"But the people chasing us," Hank drew up short in a dead-end cul-de-sac, "aren't from that area. I think we're facing a different group. Looks like more than one group wants what we're trying to find."

Two men dropped from the rooftop using an extending grapple, as the two men and two women chasing them rounded the corner, and two groups of two burst through the doors of businesses into the alley. They all drew weapons.

Chapter 8

The eight gang members circled the two, surrounding them. Their pursuers were dressed like the two people Silver had encountered at his lair. They wore black suits with white shirts, thin black ties, and polished shoes. Each attacker wore sunglasses, with the lightning bolt on a red and yellow bullseye logo of The Banzai Corporation; which showed they were tech glasses rather than normal sunglasses. And that's where the similarities ended.

"Yamaguchi-gumi," Hank said.

The eight were of Japanese descent and had a variety of weapons, including butterfly knives, nunchakus, sais, and a single naginata—a spear-like weapon with a slightly curved blade that was almost as long as its short handle.

"Why a dead-end alley, Hank?" Silver's tone was steel wrapped in irritation as he turned in a half circle, watching their assailants complete the ring around them.

"So, we can dispense with these back-alley, business-suit-wearing ninjas without any crowd interference or injuries," Hank said, putting her back to Silver and speaking over her shoulder, "to passerbys anyway."

One of the women clicked and flipped her dual butterfly knives open and closed, crouched low, and darted in, slashing sideways across Silver's midsection.

Silver's left hand moved, blocking her blade with

his own, and his right hand darted out, his wrist meeting hers and stopping her swing.

The woman reversed her strike, spinning around to slash at the tall man's face.

Before she completed her turn, Silver activated his pinky and pointer rings on his right hand. The graphene power source inside burst in conjunction with the magnetic resonator, and an arc of electricity connected the two pieces of jewelry to create electric knuckles.

The woman completed her turn, and Silver dropped into a squat, avoiding the wide sweep of her blade, and delivered two quick jabs to her midsection. The electric knuckles burst into a flare and the woman flew back and hit the alley wall.

The man with a pair of sais paused to activate his Banzai tech lenses. He drew his weapons, spun them on his fingers in a figure-eight pattern, and squared off with Hank.

Hank knew the device the man wore over his eyes could protect him from bright lights, collect and receive data about items in their field of vision, as well as assist with targeting vital areas.

The archeologist stuffed her hand into one of the many pockets on her vest and pulled out a black metal rod, about ten centimeters long. Pressing the button on one end, it emitted the high-pitched keen of an electromagnetic pulse, and then a dozen popping noises came from around the alley.

Silver's rings went dead, and his contacts faded back to normal. The man in front of Hank tore his lenses off and stared at them for a moment before throwing them to one side, and a few of the other attackers looked at the technological devices they had been preparing.

All had been rendered useless.

"You know," Silver muttered over his shoulder, "I was using that."

"Yeah, I know," Hank watched the attackers in front of her, not turning to Silver, "but they were using their toys, too, and now no one can use their toys. Well, except me. I keep mine in a Faraday bag, and they should be okay."

"At least it didn't take out the lights," Silver said, rain running down his smooth head and across his face, "I'm pretty sure a few of these guys have had some T.A.L.O.N. Agency work done and have had some lowlight genetic mods triggered."

The mini EMP sounded again, and the lights attached to the sides of the buildings in the alley, which shed dim illumination, popped and the area went dark, everything still and silent.

"Aw, dammit, Hank," Silver moaned.

"Oops," Hank felt Silver's shoulder tense against her back, "sorry."

A shout from one attacker broke the silence and was joined by the others. It echoed off the walls, making the eight sound like more. The cloud-covered sky offered no more illumination than the now-dead light bulbs, and Silver and Smith were effectively blind.

The sound of the Asian street-warriors charging filled the alley. Silver felt a sai hit his ribs, bouncing off the armored vest under his shirt, and another hit the bracer on his right forearm.

Silver punched out, blindly. His fist met no resistance. Swinging again, he clipped someone, but with little effect.

Crouching, the whoosh of nunchakus swept past

his ear, then caught him in the jaw, knocking him onto his butt.

Hank heard the clicking of another butterfly knife approaching her. She turned her head to better track the sound and felt a blade cut into her shoulder. She yelped and grabbed at the wound, feeling blood well between her fingers.

Silver hit Hank's knees from behind as he fell backwards under a flurry of blows, causing her to tumble on top of him, both falling to the ground in a heap.

The attackers rushed forward, crowding around their prone quarry, kicking, punching, and slamming weapons down repeatedly.

Silver lashed out with his twin swords, swearing, trying to hit any of the gang…with little success.

Hank curled into a ball, covering her head with her arms, shouting in pain with each blow that landed.

An attacker said something in Japanese. The beating slowed and then stopped.

"What is who doing here?" Hank said, translating what the attacker said.

A light appeared. It shone from a disc attached to the alley wall, casting bright white light across the scene.

A young man in a baggy black t-shirt and black jeans, with raven-colored tousled hair and olive skin, stood under it, drawing his hand away from the device. He had a nervous and worried look on his face.

The attackers glanced in that direction, squinting in the light.

Silver took advantage of the distraction. From his prone position on his back, he kicked out, his foot connecting with the kneecap of the woman with the butterfly knives who he'd launched into the wall a minute ago. With a crunch, she went down.

Hank drew out a zip strip and pulled it around the ankles of two distracted gang members standing beside one another, binding their legs together. Grabbing the thick piece of plastic with one hand, she punched the man on the right in the groin.

As he bent over, clutching at his crotch, Hank delivered a precise uppercut to his chin, and pulled the zip strip towards her. The man fell backwards and unbalanced the second man, falling atop the first.

Hank and Silver rose to stand, Silver putting a hand to Hank's shoulder to steady himself.

Hank looked over at him; Silver was bleeding from a cut on the back of his head, clutching his ribs, and favoring one leg.

Two of the yamaguchi-gumi members nearest the light stepped towards the newcomer, the remaining three turning their attention back to Silver and Hank.

The stranger pulled a length of lead pipe from behind him; it appearing as if from thin air. He leapt towards the two gang members with a war cry that came out as more of a high-pitched squeal, with his voice cracking in the middle.

His attack took the gang member with the nunchakus by surprise, catching the man on his jaw. The man's head snapped to the right, three teeth glinting in the air as they spun away from the jaw broken under the lead pipe's attention.

The newcomer squared his feet to shoulder-width, spread his arms out wide, and twirled the pipe at his side, twisting his wrist in a tight circle, ready for the next foe.

All the fear had disappeared, and he had a look of

steel in the set of his jaw and a flash of anger in the squint of his eyes. It was as if the man had forgotten to be meek, and some older instinct took over.

The remaining yamaguchi-gumi member spit on the ground and rushed at the disheveled youth jabbing with his short-hafted naginata.

The youth stood his ground as the gang member closed in. He swung his lead pipe at the bladed weapon, knocking it to one side. The gang member twisted the blade, bringing it back, and it bit into the youth's shoulder.

The young man's face tightened, looking decades older for a moment, and he swung the pipe again. This time upward to connect with his attacker's chin without flinching from the wound in his shoulder.

The other man's head jerked skyward, his eyes rolled back into his head, and he fell to the ground.

Hank pulled out a device with a 'Y' shaped wire. One end connected to a small black box, and the other two had sharp prongs that resembled the end of a meat thermometer. She jabbed these two ends into the thigh of each of the gang members with the zip-tied ankles and then flicked a switch on the black box.

The two men shouted as the metal leads bit into their legs, then spasmed with stifled cries, stopping their struggle to rise as their backs arched and bodies went stiff. The sais and butterfly knife clattered to the asphalt.

Silver sprung to his feet, his fist connecting with the chin of the man swirling nunchakus in a spiral. The man flew back, his head cracking against the wall, and his weapon flew to one side. He slid to the ground, dazed.

Weaving around the blunt metal sais, Silver

ducked and moved forward to the man on the ground, jamming an open palm under his chin and making his head jerk back and hit the pavement with a thud.

Silver flipped the blades in his hands and slid them back into the sheaths under his jacket and on his back.

Climbing to her feet, Hank faced the woman spinning a set of nunchakus through the air. Smiling, the woman advanced. Two polished black wooden rods connected by a twelve-centimeter chain whirled back and forth between the two women.

Hank's mind clicked through options, filtering through possibilities of behavior and reactions based on what she knew about this woman, her group, gang tactics, women in male-dominated cultures, and a few other factors. Options, like dozens of movies on fast forward, flitted through her head, until she nodded, agreeing with the most likely one and set her feet even and set her lips in a tight line.

The woman rushed forward, air whooshing around the weapon as it spun in another figure eight, then whipped back under the woman's left arm, shot forward into another figure eight, and then tucked under the right armpit.

Diversion and intimidation, Hank thought, *we're not going to fall for that, are we?*

Hank dashed forward, grabbing the woman's wrist and trapping the hand holding the weapon against the woman's chest.

The woman's left fist darted out, catching Hank in the temple and knocking her back.

Hank flailed and stumbled to one side, but she grabbed the chain of the nunchakus, yanking them from the woman's grasp, flinging them across the alley and behind a pile of loose trash.

Regaining her balance, Hank felt Silver's strong hand steady her on her right. The newcomer stood on her left. The three turned to face the last gang member, the now-weaponless woman.

"Run," Hank whispered to the woman, "get away as fast as you can, before we decide to take further steps to make sure you don't ever bother us again."

The woman turned and ran, leaving her dazed and unconscious companions behind.

"We should get out of here before these guys wake up," Silver's hand was still on Hank's shoulder, and he tugged on it, "or more show up."

"I can help with that," the newcomer's face changed as he spoke, the age melting away, replaced with a youthful nervousness and exuberance, "follow me."

Chapter 9

The young man turned and pulled open a door. Silver and Hank exchanged glances. Silver shrugged and jerked his head in the stranger's direction. Hank sighed without making a noise and nodded.

The olive-skinned man held the door open behind him, already halfway into whatever place of business it led to. Silver gestured Hank to go before him, turning to regard the stirring forms in the alley.

Hank wasn't sure if it was common sense, chivalry, or protectiveness that made Silver indicate for her to go in before him. Thinking about it for a moment, she concluded it wasn't any of those things, or perhaps a blend of all three. Silver may be protecting her, but she may be leading the way into another danger, ambush, or worse. By letting her go first, he showed either she could handle herself, or that he thought that the greater danger was behind them.

Silver watched the scattered group of gang members. They stirred, rubbing at various body parts; one at their lower back, another at their shoulder that may have been dislocated, three at head wounds, and the other two just beginning to come to consciousness.

Silver reached up to the brick wall beside the door Hank had just passed through and covered the light with his hand. The alley fell into gloom, bright triangles of white contrasting the shadows made by his hand. He pulled the light from the wall, and it winked out, casting the cul-de-sac into darkness.

"If I see your faces again," Silver growled into the dark, "I'll make you wish I never had."

"Stop threatening those poor bastards," Hank's voice drifted back from inside the building. "They probably won't even remember you talking to them. Just leave them be and come on."

Silver glanced over his shoulder towards her voice. Shoving the light into his jacket pocket, he glared into the alley. His eyes hadn't adjusted to the dark, but he thought some of them had night vision ability and might see his threatening look.

"You've been warned. Stay away," he blurted into the murky haze of the rainy night, then went into the building and pulled the door shut.

The hallway was lit by dim overhead lights, every fourth florescent fixture having two of four bulbs glowing. It cast a wane pall across the dun-colored walls and slate gray floor. The aroma of coffee hung in the air, even though the place was deserted.

The trio passed unisex bathrooms and entered the front of the business, A long, beige service counter was on one side, and framed photos of dark brown beans and burlap sacks hung on the upper half of the walls and in boxed off areas of the wainscoting covering the lower half of the walls.

Small, round tables were arranged in the center of the floor. A row of stools sat under the wrap-around sideboard, which lined the floor-to-ceiling windows that looked out onto the street, as well as the walls that were not dominated by the employee counter.

"You didn't have to threaten them." Hank glanced around the room without turning to Silver.

"Yeah," Silver leaned over the counter, checking behind it, "but I wanted to. It felt like the situation needed closure, and a threat just felt right at the time. Know what I mean?"

"All part of your plan?" Hank smiled. "How's that working out?"

The three turned to look at one another; Hank in the center of the coffee shop, Silver in front of the counter, and the stranger standing with his back to the double glass doors that opened onto the street. They sized one another up, each waiting for someone else to speak.

The lighting inside the shop was dim, with only safety lights illuminating the interior. A few people rushed past outside in the rain, not noticing the trio inside.

"Who are you?" Silver asked, leaning against the counter and crossing his arms across his chest.

"Why did you help us?" Hank said in the same moment, her hands going to her hips.

"Do you know what is happening?" the stranger asked at the same time, looking back and forth between the two, his face nervous and worried.

The words collided with one another, tangling and tumbling together. The looks on each of their faces said that part of each question had been understood, but not all of any one query.

The stranger held up a hand, stopping Hank and Silver from speaking again.

"I am Saman Kazemi, and I will answer all your questions," the newcomer held his hands at his sides, his palms outward, "I came to your rescue because I need your help."

"Well," Silver said, "ain't that something? A rescue, huh? I don't know if I'd go that far. You helped, sure, but I think we would have done just fine if you hadn't shown up."

"Silver," Hank laid a hand on her partner's arm, "I think we should let him talk. Allow him to say what he has to say without interrupting him."

The woman gave Silver a meaningful look, her head tilted and her eyebrows up, making sure he understood her unspoken context.

Hank had an incredible knack for instinctive insight; Silver had seen it at work more than once since they met a few weeks before. He'd seen her read stony-faced porters, cranky shopkeepers, suspicious customs agents, and others, and every time she'd come out on top. He was smart enough to let her take the lead in an area where he wasn't as capable.

"Yeah, whatever," Silver turned towards Saman, "go ahead then, kid, tell us what you need us to know."

"Thank you." Saman bowed his head slightly to Silver—his hands coming together in front of him, fingertips touching—and then turned and did the same towards Hank.

"Mister Silver," Saman began, "you are correct to be worried about who you can trust. There are layers of deception and many powerful people who want what you seek."

"Wait a second here," Silver stepped forward, his hand coming up and an accusing finger pointing at Saman, "how do you know what we're looking for?"

"Shh," Hank looked at Silver again, "let him talk."

"It's okay, Mz. Smith," Saman held his hands in front of him, "I understand Mister Silver's anger and concern."

"I'm not angry," Silver said, but Saman continued, interrupting him.

"You seek a great artifact, one that can mean

power just by owning it, but it really is much more to those that seek it." Saman turned and paced, his hands clasped behind his back, his shoulders hunching, and his small frame curling into itself.

"I know the Jazeer's Light," the man continued, "because my employer also seeks it. I was the one who sent the two people to your warehouse, Mister Silver."

"You sent them?" Silver took a step towards the younger man, his hands coming up in front of him, as if reaching for Saman.

"Yes," Saman turned to look at Silver, his eyes settling on the larger man's hands. His head tilted, as if he was trying to decide on the bounty hunter's intention.

"It was I who sent them." Saman raised his gaze to meet Silver's.

Silver met the younger man's eyes, and something sparked there for a moment. A hidden source of power and drive gleamed in Saman's eyes before he turned back to Hank.

"I sent two of my most trusted agents, friends, to speak with Mister Silver," Saman explained to Hank, his eyes holding hers, "but they were unable to talk to him. The whole building exploded."

"Yeah," Silver rubbed the back of his neck, looking to one side, "sorry about that."

"It is okay, Mister Silver," Saman smiled up at Silver, white teeth gleaming, "the two agents are fine. They were able to escape instead of dying. The wisdom of Ahura Mazda showed them a way out before Angra Mainyu could steal their lives.

"So, let us set aside our past differences," Saman continued, looking back to Hank who nodded at him, "and see if we can help one another.

"I know the location of the Jazeer's Light," Saman held up a hand to stop Silver's interruption, "but I want you to understand what it is before you attempt to recover it."

Both Silver and Smith nodded to Saman before he continued.

"The lamp is much more than just some antiquity of a past age, much more than some trinket meant to burn oil," Saman paused, looking at his guests before continuing, "myth and legend says it is the home to a powerful djinni, a genie in your stories."

With a click of thick paper, Saman produced an index card from thin air, held aloft between two fingers.

"And I have its current location right here."

"Do you really think he meant it's a genie's lamp?" Silver turned in the car's seat to look at Hank, the leather creaking under him.

"He told you that's what he meant," Hank let out an exasperated breath, "all three times you asked him."

The two sat in a nondescript silver coupe across from a three-story building on the corner of Gerrard Street and Wardour Street in London's Chinatown. The bottom floor housed a Chinese restaurant and a laundromat, but the two floors above were an opulent den of the Yamaguchi-gumi, disguised as a massage parlor and a series of business offices.

Wax paper lanterns hung above the street, LED lights glowing from within. At almost two A.M., only a handful of people were out on the street. A couple in a doorway, their affection for one another distracting them from anything else. A man stood under the canopy outside the restaurant, thick smoke lazily winding upward from the large cigar in his hand. The last two people had their heads down in the waning drizzle, walking in opposite directions on opposite sides of the street.

"I don't know," Silver turned back to the road, watching for anything suspicious, "I've seen a lot of things in my time, but I've never seen anything like a mythical being who grants wishes."

"It doesn't matter what you haven't seen. Others have seen unexplainable things. *I've* seen weird things in my business," Hank confided, "the earliest when my father took me to a museum exhibit when I was a kid."

Silver scoffed. "You're still just a kid."

Hank glared at Silver.

"Ok, sorry," he said with a wave of his hand, "carry on."

"Well, I was about nine years old, if that helps you, and there was a bronze kukri, an almost boomerang shaped knife from ancient Nepal. It was on display with a burial urn," Hank leaned forward and scanned the rooftops, recalling the events of that day, "which held the remains of the priest who'd used the knife in countless rituals and ceremonies, many of which probably included sacrifices and whatnot.

"We spent the whole day wandering through the museum, lingering at this display, or that exhibition. My father loved the old Greek room, talking for over an hour about the architecture and how it tied to the art, philosophy, and political climate of the era, but I kept on returning to that one exhibit with the kukri."

Silver cocked his head, his eyebrows raised, and his forehead wrinkled as he watched the young woman.

"Don't pressure me," Hank said, the corners of her mouth quirking upward. "I'm getting to it. You have to build the tension in these sorts of stories, otherwise they're just dull regurgitation of something mundane."

Hank straightened in her seat, holding her hands in front of her, gesturing as she described the next part of the event.

"For weeks following, my hands shook whenever I thought of that exhibit, and it made my head swim and my heart race. I didn't know what was going on, but I knew that there must be a reason.

"Finally, I decided I had to do something about it. I couldn't get it of my mind. I ducked out of me da's house, not that he wasn't still married to me ma, but anyway, I snuck out and went to the museum. I went in just before closing, and hid behind some concrete re-creation of a tomb, waiting for the guards to shut off the lights and settle down for the night.

"It wasn't like in the movies. You didn't have a couple men watching screens for movement, and one guy sleeping in a chair near the Egyptian wing. They locked down the building, set the sensors on the doors and windows, and then two men settled into a guard hut by the entry driveway for deliveries. Every forty-five minutes or so, one of them would make rounds around the building, using the keys to go inside, if needed.

"So, essentially, I had free run of the building as long as I didn't open a door or a window.

"It was spooky, I'll admit to that, and my imagination wanted to see shadows moving and mummies coming to life in the corners, but my logical brain knew that would be silly and shut that down quick.

"I crept through the place, because though I knew there wasn't any guards, back then I was much more scared and cautious about breaking the rules."

"I see you got over that," Silver said, bringing his lukewarm cup of coffee to his mouth.

"Oh, yes," Hank laughed, "in a big way. But don't distract me from the story. When I finally made my way to the room with the artifacts that hadn't left my thoughts in almost a month and laid eyes on that knife…"

Hank's eyes grew distant, staring at a neon sign, the light from it flooding her vision as her head was flooded with memories.

"You can't just stop there," Silver jostled her with an elbow, "go on, what happened?"

"I could swear," Hank spoke in short, quiet bursts, "the thing was glowing. Just slightly. If it wasn't dark, I don't think I would have noticed it. And I reached for it, and I did it so slowly.

"Looking at this weapon from centuries past, it filled my whole field of vision. It was like looking at a coiled snake, or standing at a clifftop and looking down, when you know something is dangerous, but you still want to get closer, to find out why it's dangerous, or if it isn't really dangerous at all. Often, something isn't really dangerous once you know more about it. Ignorance is the danger, not whatever it is you're looking at.

"But just looking wasn't enough for me. I had to touch it. I stood in front of it for almost ten minutes, just staring, leaning in, studying it with my heart racing and my mouth dry from nervousness. It beckoned to me, but not with sound or anything like that. It was just a fascination holding my attention. Then I reached out and touched it, real swift like, doing it before I could let my common sense talk me out of it."

Silver listened, sipping on his coffee, watching the building across the street as rain spattered on the windshield. He looked over when Hank fell silent.

"Well," Silver raised his eyebrows and thrust his head forward, "what happened then?"

"I don't know," Hank shrugged.

"What?" Silver's brows fell, his forehead furrowing. "What do you mean, you don't know?"

"I woke up at home," Hank sighed, as if missing a long-lost friend, "grounded, and in big trouble with my parents.

"I swear it moved towards me though," Hank said. "I mean the kukri when I reached for it. I distinctly remember it sliding closer to my hand when I reached for it. And I had a small slice across three fingers. Not deep enough to bleed, more like a light paper cut.

"I don't know what actually happened that night in the museum," she continued, "and my parents say I blacked out from adrenaline and stress. The cut on my fingers was waved off as not important, but I know something happened there."

The two exchanged glances, Silver's face neutral.

"You don't believe me, either," Hank sounded more amused then upset, the corners of her mouth turning upward, "do you?"

"Actually," Silver said, setting his cup into one of the many holders designed for that purpose, "I do. I've seen a lot of weird things in my time. Much too much to just discount anything offhand."

The two fell silent, watching the rain and the few

people out in it.

After a couple minutes passed, Hank spoke.

"What about you?" she asked.

"Hm?" Silver looked at the woman.

"I told you why I got into archeology," Hank explained, "but what about you? Why'd you get into being a bodyguard?"

"I'm not a bodyguard, per se," Silver straightened and turned towards the younger woman, "though it's one of the things my job may entail. I'm a mercenary, and a bounty hunter. I protect people, and sometimes hunt down other people."

"Yeah," Hank's mouth quirked upward, a mischievous twinkle in her eyes, "so why did you become a bodyguard?"

Silver sighed, turning away from her.

"It had to do with what happened to my family." Silver stared at the building they were staking out.

He trailed off, leaning forward and staring at something.

"Yeah," Hank said, "go on."

"Yeah," Silver's reply was short and crisp, "we need to go."

He reached for the door handle, swinging the door open into the road. A car's electronic horn blared a song lyric as it swerved to avoid the obstruction and the man leaping from the car.

"Muzzle flash," Silver growled back into the open door at Hank, "from a gun going off, I saw it in the dark room upstairs. Someone's hitting the mob we're supposed to be hitting."

He turned, slamming the car door, and moved into the street. He stopped to avoid running in front of a car, slapped the trunk as it moved past him, and bolted to the sidewalk.

Chapter 10

Hank harrumphed. She grabbed her gun case, threw open her door, and pushed up from her seat. Her seatbelt caught her and threw her back against the seat.

She growled, unclipped the seatbelt, and stepped into the rain with care. Looking over the bonnet of the car, she saw Silver run into the alley next to their target building.

She moved around the vehicle, looking left and right, and darted across the street.

Entering the alley, Hank removed a section of her gun case, leaving a handle-shaped hole. She pulled a second piece free of the case and slid the shoulder stock into the rifle grip.

She loped down the alley, spotted an open doorway on the left, and peeked in and saw Silver bounding up a set of stairs.

"Men, always so reckless," she grumbled, bolting after him.

Pulling a barrel free of the case, she magnetically attached it to the grip and stock, twisting it to lock it in place.

She moved up the stairs, stopping at the double back and pressing her shoulders against the wall. Leaning forward to look up the gap, she saw Silver a floor above her, but no enemies. Pushing off the wall, she continued her pursuit.

Hank pressed a release on the case and it lost its shape, becoming a bandolier of cartridges. She whipped it around her waist, and it magnetically caught, becoming a belt. Grabbing the remaining trailing section, she tossed it over her shoulder, and it clipped into place automatically, creating an over-the-shoulder ammo bandolier.

She pulled a cartridge from the belt and slapped it into her rifle, pressed the stock to her shoulder, and sighted down the barrel, side-stepping up the last flight of stairs, moving slower as she moved out of the stairwell and into a room.

Silver stood in the center, a lone automatic pistol held in both hands at arm's length; he turned in a slow circle. Dim light from outside the window layered the room in shadows and neon.

A dozen bodies lay in various positions, glistening pools spreading outward from their contorted forms, speaking of the violence that had filled the room. A safe stood open on one side of the room, the door swinging slightly.

"They got them," Silver muttered.

"Who got them?" Hank whispered back.

"We did," said a familiar, smoky voice. A female figure rose from a crouch next to the window, holding two pistols, one pointed at each of them, "and once again, what you sought is now mine."

"Joan?" The muzzle of Hank's gun dropped a hand-span as she stared at the woman who had once been her partner.

"You got it, babe." Joan's leg twitched, and a small dark disk slid to the center of the room. "So, you hooked up with that guy from the tomb in China?"

"It…it's not like that," Hank stuttered.

"Oh, for heaven's sake," Silver whipped his pistol towards the woman that tried to kill him a few weeks ago.

"Uh, uh," Joan thumped her chest, a blue light coming to life on her webbed harness and the disk in the center of the room, "save your ammo, hero. You're about to have lots of company and you'll need it."

The small circular object on the floor erupted in a high-pitched keening whine and flared a blue-white light.

A gun fired and glass shattered on the far side of the room.

Spots danced before Silver's and Hank's vision, and when their eyes cleared, Joan's legs were disappearing out of the top of the broken window.

Silver ran to the window, wobbling—the sound from the disk interfering with his equilibrium—and thrust his upper body out into the rain to get a shot at their escaping rival.

Joan rose upward, a magnetic hover-harness carrying her higher towards a silent vehicle that used a larger version of the same technology. A bulging knapsack bounced on her back.

Silver took aim.

The window frame beside his head exploded as a bullet from inside the room missed its target.

Looking back, Silver saw Hank diving for cover, and a dozen people filing through another doorway, weapons ready.

Silver crouched, glancing out the window.

Joan disappeared into the hover vehicle, and it zipped off into the rain with a gentle hum.

He dropped to the floor and rolled behind a desk to one side, so he wasn't silhouetted in the window's light.

The disk on the floor burst with light again.

Hank and Silver were behind cover and weren't caught in the flash.

The newcomers threw their arms across their faces, stumbling.

The keening renewed, and the men and women flooding into the room pressed their hands to their ears.

"Come on," Silver, from behind the cover of the desk, waved to Hank, "let's get out of here! We'll have to get that info some other way!"

"Set it up, laddie," Hank's brogue thickened; she was distracted, pulling a device from her harness and cobbling pieces together. "I'll be right along. I need about forty-five seconds."

Hank threw herself flat on the floor, grabbed the flash-bang disk and wormed backwards behind the couch she'd hidden behind when the yamaguchi-gumi gang members began pouring through the doorway. The device went silent and dark.

"What the hell are you doing?" Silver did a double take, his hand slowing as he pulled a flat metal square from a pouch.

Hank waved a hand at him, dismissing his question.

Silver squinted at her and cocked his head before turning to look at the gang members.

They were still stumbling into the room, holding their heads.

"Agatha," Silver said to his left wrist, "I need a car out front now. Authorize extra payment."

"Understood," came the mature female voice, the cardphone blinking green.

Silver turned back to the window, slapped the metal square on the sill, and pinched opposite sides of it. Metal claws popped out, biting into the wooden and stone wall below it.

Pinching the other sides of the gizmo, a small, circular turret popped up in the center of the square. Spinning it, so an opening within the turret pointed out of the window, Silver angled it down and pressed a button beside the round protuberance.

With a pop and a hiss, a dart—with a fine filament wire attached—shot out and sunk into the wall across the alley, unwinding the metal cord behind it. Silver pressed the same button again, and the cording wound in, drawing taut.

"Come on," Silver shouted, turning back to Hank.

"Hold on, almost there." Hank was hunched over a daisy-chained series of cardphones, each blinking a different color in a pattern that drew the eye. "Keep them busy just a wee bit longer."

Bullets whizzed by, making Silver crouch lower, as the gang members regained their senses and opened fire.

Dropping prone, Silver thrust his arm forward under the desk, and began squeezing off measured patterns of fire from his weapon.

Pop, pop. A scream and a thud as someone dropped to the floor. Pop. Another scream and shouts of pain.

Silver fired at feet, using the backlighting from the room behind the Yamaguchi-gumi members to choose his dark targets. He took his time, moving his firearm just a smidge or two each time to a new target.

A thud beside Silver made him jerk. His head hit the underside of the desk, and his vision swam—a blurred image of Hank beside him.

"Oh," Hank grimaced and patted Silver's head,

"that's gonna lump."

Silver smacked her hand away, touched his head, and winced.

"Are ye ready to go, Silver?" Hank grinned and jerked her head sideways towards the rain-soaked windowsill.

"Yeah," Silver holstered his weapon, and pulled a pressure clamp from a pouch.

The sound of electronic laughter, quiet and tinny, issued from a half dozen places in the room. Silver looked at the computer on the desk as he stood and saw cats with animated laughing faces filling the screen. Glancing around the room, he saw similar images on the phones of the wounded people on the floor.

"I'm going out that window," he said, talking quickly, "low and fast, you come right after and just grab onto me."

Hank's eyes widened and her mouth opened, but Silver leapt out the window before she could speak.

She followed, throwing herself out and grabbing at him, hanging from the tension wire.

Silver hung from the wire with one hand, gripping the pressure clamp. When Hank grabbed on, he thrust his other hand up to support the sudden increase in weight.

Relaxing his grip, Silver began their descent.

Hank looked behind them, and up at the window they had escaped through. She let out a shout of warning as one of the Yamaguchi-gumi cut the metal wire with a survival knife. The filament jerked and went slack.

The two plummeted, the wire jerking sideways when they reached the bottom of the falling arc.

Letting out a squeak in surprise, Hank's breath

caught before it turned into a scream.

Silver gritted his teeth to stop himself from biting his tongue if they hit hard. Pulling his legs to the left, he maneuvered their fall into a smooth swing.

Hank watched four gang members crowd into the window, and then pulled her knees up and hunched her shoulders, trying to hide behind Silver, as the Yamaguchi-gumi began firing at them.

Silver's feet caught a fire escape, and he pushed away, bullets ricocheting off the metal. Chunks of brick exploded as bullets missed them.

Chapter 11

He swung them fast and hard towards the street outside the alley. The wire caught the corner of the building and jerked them around it and out of sight of the mobsters.

Silver released the pressure on the grip, and the two of them slid down the wire and landed on the sidewalk, Silver on his feet, and Hank holding onto him, her eyes clenched shut and her knees pulled up to her chest.

He reached down and put a hand under each of Hank's armpits and lifted her up in front of him.

She remained in a tight ball, clutching at his clothes.

When Silver gently shook her, she opened her eyes.

"Our cab is here," Silver smiled. His teeth appeared extra pearly against his dark skin in the rain.

"Cab?" Hank looked around, dropping her legs to touch the ground. She self-consciously brushed at her wrinkled and dusty clothes.

People crowded in bunches, staying away from the alley where the gunfire had been, staring at the pair, who'd suddenly appeared from the city's dark orifice.

Silver reached past Hank and opened the door of a black cab. He waved her in.

The archeologist scooted across the back seat, hitting a magnetic release on her bandolier, and another on the weapon she carried. The gear collapsed into a pile of components as she settled into the seat. She clicked them back together into the shape of the compact briefcase before the driver could notice.

"What happened out there?" The plump, unshaven, middle-aged cabbie asked, staring out his window and up towards where they had first appeared, swinging into the street on a wire.

"Elevator was out," Silver smiled, settling into the seat and shutting the door. "We had to take a fire escape."

Hank rolled her eyes at Silver, looked down at her phone, pulled up the screen, and began sorting through the information she'd stolen.

The cab swung into traffic, accelerating with a hum and weaving around a clump of late-night bicyclists. The name on their backs showed a bright rainbow on fire, and in a block font underneath were the words, 'Burning Hope Bicycle Club'.

Midnight bike clubs had become a thing in the late thirties as more inner-city bike lanes appeared. The clubs tooled around town in sleek bodysuits, tear-drop shaped helmets, and heads-ups display glasses.

Most only had a dozen or so members, but some of the larger clubs had fifty or more. They'd spin through the city, stopping at bars, and once drunk, causing civil disturbances. Some even carried stun sticks and imposed their claim on territories through force. Club wars were on the rise again.

The graphene bodysuits provided some protection and could be wired and charged with devices ranging from stun skin protection to jump reviving an unconscious wearer with a short electrical burst.

The bicycle clubs attracted the attention of the

authorities when they got too rowdy, but they weren't easy to catch. They'd split up and take side streets, and bicycles were quieter than electric cars. They could also pick up their collapsible, metal-alloy composite bikes and walk into a building.

"Where to?" The cabbie asked, the sound vibrating and echoing through the speakers set up to deliver his voice from the front compartment to the passenger compartment in the vehicle's rear. His eyes scanned the panel of dashcams, which showed the back compartment, the road behind them, and other views.

Silver leaned forward slightly, opening his mouth to speak, but was interrupted by Hank.

"Greece," Hank cut him off, grabbing Silver's arm.

Her voice was excited, and he turned to her. She was staring at her cardphone, thumbing through pages of information.

"What?" the cabbie and Silver asked in unison.

"I haven't gone through it all," she continued as if the men hadn't spoken, "but the info I got points to Greece."

"How do you know?" Silver turned in his seat to face her.

"I started searching for references to Joan before I even had gotten settled in my seat, and something popped up. It appears the Yamaguchi-gumi had records on her, and it looks like she's employed by the Ambrose Auction Company out of Thessaloniki, Greece at the moment. The primary competitor for this artifact is the Sicilian mob family, the Russos."

"I don't go to Greece," the cabbie interjected smoothly, his voice amused, "but I can get you to the airport."

"Okay." Silver held a finger up to Hank and turned to the cabbie, looking through the window between the front and back of the vehicle. "Take us to Logan Airfield. It's about two hours northeast of London. I'm pinging the address for you now."

"That's a bit out of my area, pal." The driver raised his eyebrows into the cam.

"I'll compensate you for the time," Silver said dismissively, "dropping the tip into the e-kitty now, and it'll go through upon arrival at the airport."

Silver flipped off the intercom between the two compartments.

The car turned onto a main road and began its journey to the airport.

"Hank, we're going to need to learn more about the bad guys," Silver said in a drawn out sarcastic tone, turning back to his partner, only to be interrupted again, this time by his cardphone lighting up.

"Hold on," Silver sighed.

Hank wasn't paying much attention as she bent over her cardphone, flipping through screens of information and searching for anything that could give them further clues in finding the Jazeer's Light.

Silver switched screens from the banking app to the receive call app. Aaron Roberts's face filled the screen.

"Mister Silver," Roberts's face split into a wide smile, "I hope that this call finds you well."

"Mister Roberts," Silver said flatly, his face becoming emotionless.

The edge that crept into his voice made Hank look up.

"Tap me in," Hank said, pushing her phone

towards Silver's.

Silver pressed a button on his screen and touched the corner of his phone to Hank's. Her screen lit up with Roberts as well.

"Ah," Roberts's smile stiffened when Hank joined the call and his voice tightened, "there is the intrepid archeologist and bookworm. Greetings Mz. Smith."

"Uh huh," Hank's voice was monotone, her lips a thin line.

"I just wanted to check on your progress," Roberts's face lit up, his smile becoming easy again.

"At two in the morning?" Hank's eyes narrowed.

"Ah, yes," Roberts's camera moved, following him as he stepped back and revealing a silk robe and a glass with amber liquid, "I was up, checking on the opening of the Hong Kong markets and wrapping up some business for the closing of the New York ones, and I received a notification regarding activity here in London. Considering it had to do with quite a few mob-connected businesses having a firefight, I thought I'd call you. So, have you made any progress?"

Silver grunted at the explanation, his mind chewing on the information and comparing the flavor to his suspicious nature, which had been refined by many meals of betrayal.

"Yeah," Silver grunted this answer too, continuing with the theme and mood of the conversation. "We're following a lead."

"Oh, interesting," Roberts drained his drink and moved to a silver service trolley to refill his glass, the camera following, "and where is this lead leading?"

"Belgium," Hank said brusquely, "Brussels in particular."

Silver's head twitched, but he stopped himself

from turning to look at her.

"Brussels?" Roberts paused, pouring his drink, his head turning towards the camera. "Curious."

"Why's that? Silver asked, wondering if Roberts saw his reaction to the misinformation Hank had given.

"No reason," Roberts finished pouring the drink and lifted the glass to sip at it, staring at the camera the whole time. Pausing afterwards, he cocked his head and said, "Just unexpected, that's all."

"We'll keep you posted," Silver stated, his delivery curt and short. "We've just started planning the next step and we'll let you know as things develop."

"Yes," Roberts said slowly, moving towards the camera, "you do that. And let me know if I can offer any assistance. I have connections in nearly every country in the world, and resources that you wouldn't imagine."

"Yup," Hank said, "you'll be the first to know. And if that's all, I have work to do."

Hank thumbed her phone off, disconnecting from the call. Her face puckered into a scowl, and she paused before bringing back up the records she had hacked from the Yamaguchi-gumi.

"Well, that was sudden," Roberts smiled. "I hope I didn't upset the poor dear."

"Not at all," Silver said, his voice brightening to a cheery tone to match Roberts. "She's just focused on the job and the work, as I should be also. As she said, we'll let you know the moment we have something new. Is there anything else?"

Roberts's face was amused as he listened to the obvious dismissal.

"No," Roberts raised his glass in a toast to the

camera, "not at all. Best of luck, and here's to your continued competence and success."

The screen went black without a goodbye.

Silver's brow wrinkled. He hadn't ended the call, and Roberts hadn't reached out, or even motioned, to disconnect the communication. Was his tech that advanced that it could read his intention, or was someone else there with Roberts?

"We'll need supplies before leaving," Hank's comment interrupted his thoughts.

Silver looked at her, pulling his attention away from their benefactor. She hunched over her phone, fingers sliding across the display, highlighting clumps of information and moving it to a note-taking app.

"Don't worry," Silver looked down at his own device, pressing the screen to bring up what he had been working on before the call. "I have a plan."

He keyed a few things into his phone, then paused, tilting his head in thought.

"I've ordered a week's worth of clothing delivered for both of us, including one nice outfit, and PPE. Can you think of anything else?"

"PPE? What's that?" Hank asked without looking up.

"Personal protection equipment," Silver said, also without looking up, "so things like an undervest for me, knives and ammo for you, that sort of thing."

Hank stopped and looked at him, her brow furrowed.

"How do you know what my sizes are?" she asked.

"The usual ways," Silver huffed a laugh, "social media and a purchase-spider-crawl gets that sort of info. Thousands of advertisers have similar software to know what ads they should target you with and what to sell you."

"Ah, right," Hank gently thumped her forehead with the heel of her palm, and returned her gaze to her phone, "get me some yogurt and raisins, also, would you please?"

"Sure, I'll make sure that happens, though the search should show both of our favorite snacks, drinks, and so on."

"What happened to the car?" Hank glanced over at Silver.

Silver looked at her, then turned to glance at the driver. The mute notification was lit up on the passenger monitor screen that showed the cabbie's information, including his name, register number, speed, driving points, and so on. The man was bobbing his head to music the two of them couldn't hear through the safety glass from the back of the car, and Silver could see the man's lips moving as he sang along. For a moment, Silver wondered if the man was any good before shaking it off.

"I had it scrubbed," Silver said, looking at Hank. "I sent a code to the leasing company, and a team will be out first thing in the morning to wipe it clean. It'll be marked for sale, and people'll go look at it right where it sits, and if someone pays the money, they'll get the access code and drive it off."

"Convenient being rich, isn't it?" Hank made it a comment rather than a question with one eyebrow raised.

"It has its perks," Silver smiled wistfully.

"How do you make all that money, anyway?" Hank looked back down at her phone, trying to appear as if she wasn't that curious, but her slow and methodical movements told Silver differently.

"It was family money," he began, and it felt like the beginning of a story, the start of something he avoided telling her before they went into the building twenty minutes ago, "at least it was in the beginning. And that was an endless thing. But I turned away from it, feeling I didn't deserve it, feeling I should earn my own money.

"I was already doing the bounty hunter thing, and I continued it when I got here. I lived cheap, especially since my fees often include expenses. I could live on that and pick up a few extras with it. I invested with the rest."

"So, you're a stock market whiz in addition to a hell of a merc?" Hank glanced at him, studying him, gently urging him to tell her more, trying not to be obvious. Her sharp eyes and instinctual observation skills picked up subtle tells.

"No," Silver gave a harsh laugh, "I see things too black and white to ever be good at something like that. I had a…"

Silver hesitated and looked out the window, licking his lips.

"I have a friend," Silver continued, still staring out into the rainy night, "Jack, and he was…is…good at such things. He has a knack for knowing things and finding information."

"And did you know him before you came here?" Hank stopped messing with her phone and turned to Silver, watching him intently.

"What?" Silver shook his head, as if to clear it of the spider webs of memories, breaking his reverie. He turned to her.

"Did you know Jack before coming here from…where did you say you came from?" Hank smiled a small smile, meant to reassure her quarry, but she had that hunter's concentration now and Silver saw it.

"Nowhere," Silver's face flickered through a series of emotions—confusion, surprise, amusement—before settling into his usual guarded and stiff expression, "I didn't come from anywhere nearby. And I think that's enough of a trip down memory lane."

"Short trip," Hank muttered, looking back down at her phone.

Silver turned towards the window again, not wanting Hank to see the small smile.

Hank smiled also, watching the reflection of Silver's face in the window as they sped past streetlights.

They traveled the rest of the way to the airport in silence.

By the time they arrived at the airport, Hank had pulled enough information from the files to give them a direction to go, and Silver had ordered supplies to be delivered to his private jet at Logan Airfield, submitted a flight plan and had it approved, and both had taken a short nap.

Once on the plane, they checked their injuries, showered, and outfitted themselves.

The two settled into oversized leather captain's chairs as the pilot taxied the plane down the runway.

"So," Hank projected a map from her phone to the screen on the cabin wall, "this is the projected path. Greece first…"

A red dot appeared on the map northeast of

London, and a line traced itself eastward, heading for Thessaloniki, Greece.

Chapter 12

The gala was a dazzling event. The eighteen-person orchestra—called a chamber orchestra, Silver explained to Hank—set the tone, pace, and mood of the cavernous ballroom. Hank commented how the speed of the crowd, not just dancing, but also the ones milling about, was affected by which piece the orchestra played. The conductor appeared to be aware of how he influenced the gathering, his oiled, dark goatee twitching with a smile when he sped up the orchestra and the surrounding people also moved at a more frantic rate, only to slow and almost breathe a collective sigh when the next, slower, arrangement began.

The event took place in the arts district. They renovated the building in the 2030s. Earthquakes and the subsequent flash floods had shattered the area in the mid-2020s, not to mention what the COVID-19 epidemic did to the already injured Greek economy in the first part of the decade. After almost ten years of being a white, tattered quasi-ruin, lying on the tiered Greek hillsides like the bones of a long-forgotten monster from a long dead culture, someone with more money than sense came along and threw a couple billion into revitalizing the district. They made a mint as a result, as well as contacts with local and federal governments. Not to mention the IOUs and non-financial debt they gathered from the aforementioned entities.

The magazines and gossip columns that reported the investor had "no sense" ate crow along with their words. This spot in Thessaloniki, Greece, was now one of the most popular destination spots in the Mediterranean.

The hall that Silver and Smith walked through had high, vaulted ceilings with frescos painstakingly recreated on the domed plaster, alcoves with marble statues, and ornately gilded columns in four tidy rows along the sides and center of the room.

Silver dressed in a classic black and white tux, but with the modern stylistic twist of having no lapels, replaced with a short, starched collar that stood up along the neck. The lines of the outfit gave Silver a sleek profile, making him appear slimmer, but with taut lines of corded strength. Men and women followed his progress through the room, leaning towards one another and pointing at him, clutching champagne glasses, as they whispered theories about who he might be.

On the opposite side of the room, Hank walked along the white-clothed tables holding an endless array of finger foods. She wore a pale grey pantsuit with silver threading that caught the light and twinkled when she turned. Her wide cuffs swirled around her ankles, giving her purposeful stride a gentler motion. The way she constantly turned her head and upper body to observe the room and people within became almost a dance as her outfit undulated with the motion.

The man they sought, Morgan Ambrose, was the one who had revitalized this area, as well as being responsible for the party. He was a middleman who made his money by creating transactions; sometimes micro transactions, other times huge ones, like buying a part of a town, rebuilding it, and donating it to the government.

On the plane, Hank told Silver about the information she found, and how it pointed to Ambrose and his operation. Well known for holding open events with secret auctions behind the scenes, he kept them hidden from the press and locals behind a smokescreen of glitz and glamour.

The morning after they'd landed and settled into a hotel, Saman showed up, casually knocking on their door. He had an air of cocky confidence that hadn't been there before, standing taller and carrying himself like he was ready to spring into action. No longer nervous, he had an almost amused air. It was quite a change from the anxious kid they met in London.

He had a five o'clock shadow of a beard, a new haircut, and new clothes. Tight and black, highlighting a runner's physique, his wiry muscles accented by the t-shirt hugging his biceps and pecs. Maybe that was it. Silver had known many men who got a bit full of themselves after a good haircut and new outfit. All in all, it made Saman appear older and more mature.

Saman told them he was there to offer whatever assistance he could; restaurants, gear, deliveries or pickups, or even to just to hail a taxi.

Silver suggested they discuss it over lunch, and to meet in the café across the street and shut the door on the young man.

After a quick discussion between Silver and Hank—a discussion that stressed suspicion and caution of someone who appeared suddenly when that person hadn't even known that they had left England—the two headed for the café.

Saman sat, legs crossed, and half reclined with one

arm over the back of the chair next to him, sipping a tiny cup of coffee so thick and dark it looked like syrup.

He gestured to chairs across from him for them to sit, an amicable smile on his face. Offering to buy lunch, he filled the time with small talk about Thessaloniki and the history of it, and Greece in general. He spoke with expansive knowledge of the region, and went into great detail about ancient Greece, its religions, and philosophies.

When the meal ended, Saman leaned forward conspiratorially and confided that greater forces were at work here than they realized. He warned they should be cautious, and trust no one. He also promised to find more information, for their sake, about who their shadowy foes may be.

As for their part, Silver and Hank were closed lipped about what they learned regarding the auction and Morgan Ambrose, the Russo family, and Joan's connection to both.

But Saman never asked, either. He seemed to have stopped by only to socialize and offer any assistance they might need.

This, by itself, made Silver even more cautious.

It didn't go unnoticed that Saman had a half-dozen people stationed within a block of the café, watching Silver and Smith, as well as the street.

Silver nodded at two familiar people, a man and woman—her in a wrist cast, him in an arm cast and a layer of flesh-colored plasti-cast on his face—and they smiled and waved in return.

After the lunch, Silver swore people were following them, watching them from alleys and rooftops, and every store clerk and passerby were leaning in to hear their conversations.

Hank told him he was just being silly, but even she was on edge. Too many coincidences, or too many kindnesses, were too good to be true.

The pair begun their investigations, tracking the auction, and finding the information without too much trouble. A few bribes here and there, and the police fairly fought with one another to bring them new information first.

The night of the gala, they'd entered separately, ten minutes apart, with Silver arriving first. Hank followed, but in a group of local university students who showed up to receive small scholarships and grants in the field of sociology and archeology. Hank contacted the school—after learning about the outing in their four days of research—and asked to be included as a visiting student from their sister academy from Dublin, Ireland. The credentials had been a simple matter to forge for Hank, electronically creating the plasti-chip cards with her skills in documents and computers.

Silver didn't have a cover and didn't need one. He was wealthy and had considerable contacts. He simply showed interest in supporting the arts and education, contributing to the charity a small sum of $100k, and was granted entrance to the gala. It didn't allow him entrance to the auction, which apparently didn't exist according to everyone directly connected to the event, but others—not attached to the institution—said differently.

The two came together, briefly, near the expansive stretch of tables that held food. Finger foods lined white tablecloths; fountains of chocolate and caramel bracketed a pool of warm, melted marshmallow, with trays of cookies to dip into them circling around them;

a dozen varieties of shrimp set around an ice sculpture of Athena, the goddess of war and wisdom, with various dips and sauces dotting the white tablescape; finger sandwiches, cheeses, and expensive beef cubes intermingled with baked meat mini-pies, basted seasoned air-fried baby potatoes, and other delights.

Silver and Hank synchronized earbuds before entering, so didn't need to be near one another to communicate, but still held a brief conversation at the table.

But it was unrelated to their actual business here. They had a momentary disagreement about butter, Hank saying it was detrimental to the atmosphere because cattle who made methane in their natural gaseous way, and Silver, who touted the seaweed diet for livestock that solved such issues.

"Joan!" Hank hissed in Silver's ear.

He reached up to push at his ear, his face screwing into a look as he sought Hank across the crowded room.

"What?" he muttered, turning towards a potted plant with long fronded fingers standing in front of one of the ornate pillars, so no one would see him talking to himself.

"Joan is here, I just saw her," Hank's voice was urgent, then it changed to confusion, "Why are you talking to a plant? Don't you think that sort of thing might stand out?"

"What else am I supposed to do?" Silver turned, covering his mouth with a napkin. He spotted Hank and looked in her direction. "People will see me talking."

"Oh, I thought you were good at this," Hank laughed, rocking back with amusement. She held her cardphone up in front of her, looking over its rim at him. "You could just talk at your phone, like everyone else does."

Hank gestured around the room, and Silver's gaze followed. Dozens of people wandered with their phones held in front of them. Some were scrolling social media; some spoke into them, having a conversation with an image of someone who wasn't here; while others played games using eye-tracking technology to bounce the balls, click the cats, or do whatever the game offered.

"What about Joan?" Silver sighed with a shake of his head and lifted his cardphone up in front of him, eyes narrowing in irritation, even though he still held the napkin in front of his mouth. "Where is she, and did she see you?"

"No," Hank's voice sped up, redirected to the topic, "but she saw you. She's on the balcony at the head of the room—in a stunning deep sapphire evening gown, it really accentuates her form, and her hair looks dazzling in a high bun—and she's leaning on the stone railing, scanning the crowd. She looks so regal, like she's surveying her subjects at a royal ball."

"Hank," Silver interrupted, "can you cut the fashion review short and get on with it?"

"Ah, right," Hank flushed, her face becoming a deep red that Silver could see from across the room, "she spotted you and watched for a few minutes. She said something into her wrist-com, but I couldn't pick it up on mine due to all the ambient noise in here. After another thirty seconds or so, she turned and went into…uh, oh."

"What?" Silver had been looking at the balcony, studying the layout and doors on the second level that circled the ballroom floor, but turned to Hank.

She looked at him with wide eyes. Not directly at him, but behind him.

Silver turned and saw three men in cheap tuxedos. Each was probably twice as wide as him, but only one was taller. The goon squad arrived, and they headed straight for him.

Silver smiled a toothy smile at the men, a white wall of charm.

"Gentleman," Silver nodded in their general direction, "am I finally going to get the personal service I so rightly deserve?"

The three men stared at him, the one on the left with a dark furry mole on his cheek, furrowing his brow in confusion. The mole-man glanced at the other two, leaning forward to see past the middle one, trying to determine if they were expected and he'd misunderstood their directions.

The other two men showed little reaction, the taller one on the right scowled slightly, and the other, the middleman, waved one hand in the direction they'd come from, turning his body to indicate that Silver should move that way.

The other men also turned, creating a passage between their line-backer forms.

Silver moved past them, glancing at the middleman who had gestured, to see where to go next. He thought this man was the perfect blend of classic mobster and boxer, the repeatedly broken nose fitting both mental images.

The three men fell into place around him, the mole-man on the left, the middle man—well, Silver couldn't call the man 'middle-man' anymore, since the man was no longer in the middle, instead he mentally decided to call him broke nose—corrected to broke-nose, was on his right, and the third, the rather nondescript tall man, was behind him.

Broke-nose was to Silver's right and gestured again as they walked, indicating where he should go.

Silver walked like they were his personal bodyguards—which they were, in a way—with his head held high and an air of self-importance. Anyone seeing the procession would assume that the tall, fit black man bracketed by three slope-browed muscle, was guiding them, and not the other way around.

"Well, gentlemen," Silver said, his com line open and Hank listening, "looks like tiger gets to be the good sport."

The men glanced at him, confused. Mole-man even raised a finger and opened his mouth to ask a question, but was silenced by a slight glare and shake of the head from the other two.

"I told you," Hank said into Silver's ear through the bud, "don't call me sport, or tiger, or, oh, never mind."

She sighed into Silver's ear.

"Fine," she mumbled in an irritated tone, "you go hang out with the boys, and I'll go shopping. A woman's work is never done."

Chapter 13

After being led through a small maze of corridors, they took Silver to a back room. Nothing he couldn't find his way back through if he was at a casual strolling pace, but if in a running firefight, he might take a wrong turn.

He made a mental note of that as he sat in a comfortable waiting room. Well, it was a casual interrogation room dressed up to look like a comfortable waiting room. It brought images to mind of the adult interview videos of the twenty-teens. That thought made him shudder and decide to avoid sitting on the leather couch.

The men scanned Silver for contraband in the antechamber—a true antechamber: huge, stone, and two floors tall with gleaming white marble work that put modern rooms to shame—outside the room, finding and confiscating various items. They took two pens, cardphone, earcom, jacket lining flat pin gun, key fob with various digital and physical multi-tools, smart-watch with a control panel for various things, and a pack of minty gum.

They'd taken his gum.

Silver smacked his lips, suddenly really, really wishing he had a stick of gum.

How can a mouth water and feel dry at the same time?

He ran his tongue across his lips.

He circled the room, hands in his trouser pockets. They'd taken his outer coat, because of all the tech hidden within it. He wore the vest still, though, and suspenders under it. They weren't to hold his pants up, or to accent his fashion—no one would see them under his vest—but held other useful things. As did the heels of his dress shoes, and a few other things. He didn't have any tech, but he still had some basic tools and an extensive skill set.

Silver settled on the corner of the desk, half leaning, half sitting, his hands on the edges behind and to the side of him.

Looking around the room, he wondered at the lack of art, knickknacks, or paintings. It had another lone plant with long, fronded fingers that made him think of two-dimensional drawings of monsters in the dark.

The room, a bit cliché, had a long mirror on one wall. Other than the door in and out, that was the only thing on the four walls. The décor was simple: a black leather couch, a table-like desk with a chair on each side, and a low-slung, dark-colored, upholstered box chair. The table had the plug-and-play inset where someone could attach a computer.

Silver's musings were interrupted when the door opened. Turning towards it, he cocked his head in curiosity as a tall, lanky woman in a deep-red business suit entered, desk computer in hand, followed by a rough-shaven man wearing an expensive, wrinkled salmon colored suit. Silver wasn't sure if the outfit was tousled for the sake of fashion, or if the man was just slovenly.

The woman smiled at Silver, though he thought it looked more like a rictus grimace. Her black hair shone in a shoulder length page cut. Silver stared at her, something feeling off. Her hair…was crooked. So, it was a wig; he decided. Which with her social skills, stiff demeanor, and the loose cut of her outfit, Silver thought she was definitely more than a secretary. She was security.

But the man matched his suit in shade, if not color, to her much darker outfit. So perhaps a couple also?

"Richards," the man said, extending a hand to Silver, "Keith Richards, no relation. If you're even old enough to remember who that was."

"I know who that is," Silver stood and took the man's hand, shaking it three precise times up and down and releasing it, "and some folks say he's still around, one of the first to test the Tesla Eternity System."

"Yeah, I heard about that in the late twenties," the man moved to the box chair in the corner, lowering himself slowly into it with a wince and a hand on each arm of the chair, "one of Elon Musk's crazy ideas, and working with Jeff Bezos, right?"

"Yeah, that's what people say," Silver turned, watching the woman circle the desk and plug in her graphene machine, "and that they wanted to raise Steve Jobs' conscience from the computer it had been locked in with the help of Bill Gates, who was mourning the loss of his old friend."

"Oh yeah," Richards laughed, a coarse sound that spoke of years of living hard. "I forgot about all that conspiracy stuff."

The room fell silent, except for the sounds of the woman settling into her chair in front of her computer, and her nails tapping along the flat sheet keyboard.

"Transcriptionist also?" Silver asked the man, gesturing towards the woman who stared directly at him as she typed.

"Bunny is a woman of many and varied talents,"

Richards paused, leaning back, a breathy moan of discomfort escaping him, "and handles the interview processes, from recording to questioning, as well as being my personal bodyguard, among other things that have to do with my body."

Silver glanced at the woman, she was smiling a wooden smile that didn't reach her eyes, and still stared at him eerily.

"Let's hope we don't need her to do more today than just typing and talking," the host's Greek accent thickened and his eyes narrowed, "no?"

Richards leaned back into the chair, steepling his fingers in front of him, watching Silver digest the barely veiled threat.

Hank glided along, her arms swinging at her sides, making shushing noises as the material of her sleeves rubbed against her sides.

She had to hold them out slightly, accommodating the glorified fanny pack around her waist. It was a tasteful accouterment, having a large flat pocket in the back, and then two small pouch-pockets in the front, one on the left and one on the right.

She stumbled, tripping over her own feet. A strong hand reached out and steadied her. Looking to her right, she saw a man in his mid-twenties smiling at her, his hand on her elbow.

"Oh, my," Hank smiled back at the man, stumbling again and putting a hand on the man's arm to hold herself up, "I don't think I knew, that is, I've never had…"

Her words trailed off as if her mind meandered

into a dark thicket of thoughts and got lost.

"Champagne?" the man asked.

"What?" Hank's head jerked back up to the man, causing her to wobble again. She turned her head to the empty champagne flute in her hand. "No, I've had some, but thank you ever so kindly."

"No," the man laughed, his blue eyes lighting up with merriment and amusement, "I was asking if the champagne was having its way with you."

"Oh," Hank's eyes went slightly unfocused, her gaze moving from the glass to the man and back again, "I guess it may have. I've never had a glass of spirits do something like this to me, and I'm not used to anything having their way with me."

"Oh, really now?" The man's accent sounded Italian, though his dark hair and olive skin could have been from anywhere around the Mediterranean. "We'll see if we can correct that."

"What?" Hank smiled at him, her eyes coming into sharp focus on his face, and for a moment she seemed completely sober.

"Oh, nothing," the man seemed to not notice her reaction to his comment, "I was just saying that champagne isn't a spirit. Spirits are the hard alcohols."

Hank's face went still and tight, her lips pressed together. She wanted to expand on that, educate the man on the actual details and differences between spirits.

"Are you okay?" The man asked, his face noticing the change in hers.

Hank blew out a great puff of air right into the man's face, putting a little burp into it, which made him clench his eyes, wrinkle his nose, and turn away for a moment.

"Oh, yeah," Hank drawled, dragging out the vowels in the word. Her next words were clipped and broken, with a slight slur. "I am perfectly fun. I mean, fine. Mind you, I am fun, too. Well, I can be. I have some friends that say I am a bit stiff and need to relax and have fun. But I do have fin."

She paused, a surprised look on her face, as if she just heard her own words. Then she burst into laughter and thudded the champagne glass against the man's chest and ran it down along his arm to deposit in into his hand.

"I said fin, instead of fun," she laughed, "oh my, that's the spirit!"

She laughed again at her own pun and wrapped both of her now empty hands around the man's arm.

"Well, now that we've got that cleared up," she ran one hand up to his bicep, squeezing, "oh my, you work out, don't you?"

The man was bewildered and no longer in control of the conversation with the girl who'd drunkenly stumbled in front of him.

"I think it's time to go to the auction." Hank let her head fall against the man's arm for a moment before lifting it up again and extending her free arm out in front of her, pointing. "Onward Charles, into the fray!"

She walked forward, still holding the man's arm, and he followed, his face changing from confused to amused.

"You do have your door pass, or invitation, or ticket, or whatever dreadful thing they require to get in, don't you?" Hank asked, her voice steadying with each step.

"Of course I do," the man said. "Grandmother

almost pinned it to my lapel like I was in kindercare. She told me to buy something nice and expensive for my father, to help secure my future."

"Oh," Hank said, "family money, eh? Well, I had to make my money the old-fashioned way. I earned it. Which is why I drink other people's alcohol, spirits or otherwise."

"How did you know my name was Charles?" the man asked.

"What? Is it really?" Hank stopped and spun the man to face her. She burst into high-pitched laughter, poking him in the bicep with a finger, then sliding her hand onto the muscle and squeezing again, her eyes dreamy.

She shook herself and looked back up at him sheepishly.

"That was the name of my childhood pup. He was always making messes that needed cleaned up afterwards," she murmured, dropping her eyes. "Is that really your name, or are you just having a piss?"

"No," the man smiled and turned her back towards the door they'd been heading for, "it really is my name. What a happy coincidence that you would guess it like that."

"Oh yes, Charles," Hank rolled her eyes as she leaned her head against his arm and they approached the two men standing on each side of the doorway into the auction room, "quite the coincidence. Now, let's go in and see all the pretty things."

Chapter 14

The wig came off.

Not only did it come off, it flew across the room with the effort of Silver blocking the flying kick with both arms crossed in front of him in an 'x' as Bunny vaulted across the desk at him.

Silver twisted his arms, grabbing her ankles a moment after the woman's feet hit him, and swung her sideways, launching her towards the leather sofa.

The wig went in the other direction, towards Keith Richards. The man let out a scream like a rocker during the bridge of their most popular song, and swatted at what looked very much like a very large and very angry spider.

He knew it wasn't a spider. He'd watched it come off his assistant's head. But some primal instinct made him pull his legs up, cross his arms, cringe backwards, and swat at the dark object hurtling towards him with one limp hand.

Silver didn't know exactly where things went wrong. It was all going so well. Bunny asking questions woodenly and typing without looking at her keyboard; Richards grunting and harrumphing as Silver verbally slid past the questions; and Silver smiling to himself as he waxed poetic on topics not even remotely related to the questions.

Questions are easy to avoid. Silver never understood those old police TV shows from the turn of the millennia where a criminal would break down and spill the beans in front of a crowd, or a courtroom, just because someone verbally berated them.

Silver smiled and recalled cutesy anecdotes, instead of crumbling under the questions. He didn't know where it went wrong, and why it escalated so suddenly.

It may have been when Silver refused to give any information about why he was here. He'd maintained the story that he was rich and bored, which is the same story he sometimes gave when people asked why he travelled the world pursuing dangerous criminals and hunted people of interest.

Or it may have been when he suggested that Richards enjoyed the romantic company of sheep. It had been a joke, a cliché from an era gone past. But Richards was of a generation who'd been labeled a snowflake during the twenty-teens. The generation born in the 1990s or early 2000s was raised believing it was other people's job—no, not job…more like duty and responsibility—to go out of their way to never say anything that might hurt that millennial's feelings, attack their beliefs, or even disagree with them.

This made Richards tinge purple above the collar. He was not a patient man, and if Silver had to guess, also prone to high blood pressure and heart issues.

So, using the man's shading as his gauge—almost an applause meter—Silver pushed the man's figurative buttons. Right up until Richards's patience burst and the man screamed, "Kill him, Bunny! Hurt him! Punch him! Break him and make him tell us all the things!"

Silver spun towards Bunny, crouching into a fighting stance without thinking about it.

The woman bounced off the back of the couch, hit the leather seat cushions with a squeaky farting noise as her arm slid across, and hit the floor on her butt with a dull, muted thump.

Silver snorted a laugh.

Richards's trill scream, demanding Bunny do better at the violence, filled the room.

Bunny rose to her feet, but stayed low, her left leg extended in front of her with her weight on her back leg, and her arms mirroring the positioning.

Silver cocked his head and raised an eyebrow. He stood up quickly and stiffly, throwing his hands above his head, and shouting, "I give up!"

Bunny's posture relaxed, just a little bit.

Richards stopped screaming, his voice stopping as if someone used a mute button on his personal remote.

They both looked up at Silver's hands.

Silver smiled and clicked his heels together. It was an almost military movement and would've made most people think about past dictators that demanded crisp movements and immediate reactions of their soldiers that gave an almost worshiping feel.

But Silver's smile belied that impression as he clicked his heels.

His smile widened as Bunny's hands shot to her head, gripping it as she lost her balance and fell back on her rump once again.

A cha-chunk that sounded like the footfall of a giant robot in the distance accompanied an electric whine from the maglock on the door.

Richards's eyes were wide and bewildered when Silver lowered his hands and turned to look at the man.

Bunny swooned like a street fighter who had their ears boxed, causing a sudden ringing that disoriented a person. Neither Richards nor Bunny would have heard the small, localized, EMP wave that threw off electronics within a very small area.

Watching the swift movements and stunted reactions of Bunny, Silver guessed that she'd been modified. Yep, an Abbey Normal. That was the street slang for an AB Normal, or in technical terms, an Adjusted Bioengineered Normal. In other words, someone who had nanotechnology implants.

Without a second thought, Silver grabbed the potted frond-plant tree-thing and swung it at Richards's head.

In an explosion of rich, dark soil, and pale, glistening spittle, Richards collapsed in a heap.

Silver reached for the door, and the knob turned easily. Silver pulled on the handle, but the door didn't move. A quick glance told the bounty hunter that the maglock had been activated. He was trapped in this room unless he could release the mechanism before the two people came to their senses.

Hank smiled at the woman from beside Charles.

Joan stared at her, eyes narrowing, as Hank lowered herself into one of the three dozen recliner chairs in the room.

The room was a small auditorium. A stage, two steps higher than the floor, spread across one long wall. The recliners were twelve across—three, a walkway, six, a walkway, and three again—and each row was up a step and allowed people in the back to see above the heads of the people in the front.

Heavy red-velvet curtains to muffle sound hung on the walls, and vertical rectangle lights spilled a yellowed glow upward and downward to create an hourglass effect on the wall.

A small podium stood in front of another curtain on the stage.

Joan stood in the wings of the stage, to the audience's right, the stage left for those on the stage.

Two attendants circulated through the seated patrons with trays, serving drinks and more finger foods. They carried small crystal plates and cloth napkins to give to the high rollers slowly filling the seats.

Within twenty minutes everyone was seated, chatted with or ignored their neighbors, and the auctioneer mounted the stage.

He was a man well into his sixties, with rotund, wiggling jowls, and a red, patchy face. He spoke slowly and precisely, as if to mock the traditional auctioneers of old.

He pointed at an item rolled onto the stage on a silver trolley cart, asked for a price, told some tidbit of trivia or history, asked for another bid, and repeated the process.

It fascinated Hank. Though the man repeated the process almost exactly each time, it seemed as if each moment was new and different.

It wasn't fast or rushed, though the pace was steady, instead the man drew it out, making it feel languorous and decadent. The audience ooh-ed and aah-ed in the right places, accenting the man's spiel as he appeared almost bored.

Hank stifled a yawn. She could spend fourteen hours in the field, digging and dusting broken bits of time-bleached pottery shards and remain interested, but this was beyond her. She was getting sleepy.

Then the Jazeer's Light was brought on stage.

It was an ancient oil lamp from a long-forgotten era. Brass polished to a high shine, looking like a container of golden metal squashed down, then taken by spout and handle and pulled until it stretched into an elongated teapot.

Bids for previous items for sale had started around a half million dollars, give or take a hundred thousand. This one started at a million. The first bid jumped it to sixty million dollars. And so it went.

The auction drew out as the auctioneer threw out facts about the item. He mentioned it was first found in Iraq in 700 AD. It came from the Persian Empire during the time of King Cyrus. He went on, dropping hints of rumored, mysterious powers and the good fortune that came with owning it.

The crowd murmured as the man turned interesting history and facts into the mental equivalent of a mouthful of crackers being washed down with a trickle of water.

Hank sat in the front row, in the center chair, sharing the spotlight centered on the podium and the fat, sweating man. As voices raised, a sharp retort caught her attention.

Turning, without thinking, she caught sight of the other guests in the room. These were not the elite and upper crust of society.

The row directly behind her held five slim, hungry looking Asian men who leaned forward in interest, their predatory gaze glaring at the artifact.

To her right were swarthy Arabians, dressed in silk business suits, whispering to one another in their guttural language.

To her left were olive-skinned Italians, swirling ruby-hued wine in crystal-stemmed glasses with an air of relaxed arrogance. Behind them were two rows of dour looking Americans, made obvious by their monotone suits and bright red or blue neckties.

Looking over her right shoulder showed Irish mafia, dressed more like they had just come from a nightclub than like they were attending a prestigious event. Behind them in the back row were three men arguing quietly in Spanish, their accents hinting that they were from Central and South America, their attitudes broadcasting they'd only joined into an alliance to afford the object of their desire.

The back row, behind the Asians and Hank, was in shadows, but more men and women of wealth and power leaned back in those chairs, raising hands or paddles to bid on the singular artifact that was the pièce de résistance of the auction.

The Jazeer's Light.

Chapter 15

Panic rose in Silver's throat, along with bile burning his esophagus. Trapped in a room with a genetically altered killing machine, and an egomaniac who hated being denied anything, with less than a minute to find a way out before the former recovered enough to tear him apart on the behalf of the latter.

Silver wondered if the EMP locked the door. It should've released any magnetic lock, but Silver was unsure if a magnetic pulse would sever a magnetic connection or trigger it. The sound he'd heard from the door moments ago may have been the death knell of his doom.

He sighed, his shoulders slumping.

But he didn't have time for that sort of behavior. He could do that in about fifty seconds as Bunny pummeled the life out of him if he couldn't get the door open. He wondered for a brief moment, if she'd laugh manically when she did it. He doubted it, but he'd bet a dollar that Richards had a maniacal laugh or two saved up for a special occasion.

His hands slapped at his pants pockets—first the front right, then the front left, back right, back left, and then moved to pat his left breast pocket and the two vest pockets—taking inventory of what he had at his disposal. While he did, his eyes scanned the room, doing the same visually as his hands were tactilely.

He had it, his head jerking up when the thought hit him. He stopped thinking and acted.

Reaching under his vest, he moved across the room to the paper-thin graphene keyboard and monitor, unclipping the thin metal of his suspender clamps. First the front two, then the back two. At the desk, he pulled his suspenders from under his vest through a sleeve hole, like a woman removing her bra after a long day of work.

Silver pulled the metal clamps holding the suspenders to his pants from the elastic and discarded the useless material on the floor.

He lifted his right foot and removed his shoe. Holding a metal clamp open on the desk, he hammered it three times using the heel of his shoe. Once reasonably flattened, he did the same with the other side. He repeated this with the other three clamps.

Snatching the keyboard up—because that was the part that held the computer CPU, and most of the electrical current—he dropped the shoe onto the floor, shoved his foot into it, ignoring the fact that the back folded under his heel, and moved towards the door, attaching the four flattened clamps to one side of the keyboard.

Reaching the door, he held the paper-thin piece of graphene with a six-centimeter-wide aluminum strip along one side. He hoped it was thin enough.

The woman sitting on the floor was recovering. Her head was still in her hands, but she wasn't shaking it anymore, and the lack of movement allowed Silver to see her focus clearing.

Silver jammed the jury-rigged faraday cage between the door and the doorjamb. It didn't fit. He didn't flatten the metal enough.

With a flick of his ankle, his shoe came off again. Bending to pick it up, he caught the movement of

Bunny as she pushed to her hands and knees, preparing to stand up.

Snatching his shoe from the floor, Silver held the keyboard against the wall, and hammered at the suspender clamps with the heel again. The second one down broke at the spring hinge and fell to the floor. The remaining three looked like a child's grin after losing their first tooth. He slid the three together and jammed it back between the lock on the door and the wall.

It clicked.

The woman gained her feet shakily, one hand on the arm of the leather couch, her knees wobbling like a baby deer taking its first steps. Except this baby deer could tear Silver's arms from their sockets.

Bunny's chin lifted slightly, eyes hooded by her brow, and her bald head gleaming in the overhead LED lighting. There was a grimace of pain and anger on her—up until this moment—emotionless face.

She charged.

It was still a stumbling charge, like a locomotive about to go off the tracks. But a speeding train could do significant damage, whether it was on the tracks or off.

Silver—shoe in one hand, graphene keyboard in the other—pulled open the door, spun through the opening, and slammed it behind him.

He heard two noises: one was the click of the door's magnetic lock securing itself again, the other was Bunny's fist hitting the four-centimeter-thick metal door. The frame shook, and an eight-centimeter-wide bulge appeared next to Silver's face.

"See to your boss," Silver called, but not loud enough to alert anyone in nearby rooms.

He bent and put his shoe on properly, watching the door to see if Bunny would hit it again.

She didn't.

Silver moved down the hall, collected his confiscated property from a table against the wall, and dropped the ravaged keyboard behind yet another potted frond plant.

He wondered how many damn potted frond plants they had around here. But that thought was gently pushed aside as the more immediate concern of how long it would take those two to get out of the room came to the forefront of his worries.

Lights blinked. Red and white, small rectangular lights near the ceiling rhythmically pulsed.

Silver sighed again.

That would be some sort of alarm. Whether Bunny used Richards's cardphone, or had some communication implant…someone, somewhere, knew Silver was here and on the loose.

He moved quicker.

Hank hated this. All of this. Joan glaring at her. This strange man to her right, Charles, who she had to pretend to be a drunken idiot in front of to get something from him. A priceless artifact that petty people were arguing over, even killing over, because they thought it had some kind of power or prestige that would allow them to control others. The arrogant attitudes of people who thought they didn't need education because they had money.

But she loved that one thing, just in front of her and to the left. The dully gleaming trinket beside the fat, sweaty man on stage. A craftsman's project from over two-thousand years ago. An item that had been around long enough that people had placed belief and faith in it as a magical thing that could grant wishes. She loved the Jazeer's Light and everything like it.

It was that marvel of human psychology that drew Hank to archeology. The thought of something—if it was old enough—could hold wonder and awe and power.

It could be a copper chamber pot, a broken shard of pottery, a Neolithic stone arrowhead, or a piece of petrified wood from some lost and forgotten civilization before the Agricultural Revolution 10,000 years ago, and it would hold power.

What she really wanted to do was stand up, walk to the lamp, snatch it and proclaim it under her protection until she could get it safely to a museum where everyone could bask in its glory, learn its history, and gaze in wonder at the gravitas of importance that time could give such an item.

In her movie in her mind, she knew they would never let her take it. She'd have to fight her way out. She pictured leaping over a horde of swarthy men— kicking two in the faces, punching another in the throat, while cradling the lamp in the crook of her arm—and taking them down like keystone cops. The daydream faded as the red-faced man at the podium pushed the crowd for a higher dollar amount.

Small lights along the ceiling began blinking red and then white in pulsing flashes. Everyone looked up at them. Joan moving towards the auctioneer drew Hank's attention back to the stage.

"Wrap it up, fat man," Joan growled, her large hand wrapping around the sweating man's upper arm and squeezing.

"What?" the man turned and looked at Joan, his face becoming an angry maroon.

Joan glared at him, and combined with the pressure of her grip, and the glimpse of a sidearm under her dark blue dungaree jacket…the man swallowed hard.

He turned back to the room.

"Please," the man said, his voice cracking, "if I may have your attention. I am sure there is nothing to worry about. Let us return our attention to this dazzling and priceless artifact."

Having risen partially out of their seats in concern, people settled back into them. Hands slid under coats or behind their backs, and Hank realized that there was more firepower in the room than she'd thought.

"I will take final bids now," the auctioneer moaned, glancing at Joan's hand holding his arm, and then looking at her other hand under her jacket. "I believe the last bid was one point four billion dollars. Do I hear one point five billion?"

"Two billion dollars," one of the Sicilians said, standing and buttoning his suit jacket. His statement had an air of finality to it, and Hank knew the man didn't expect anyone else to counter his offer.

His men stood also, but didn't button their jackets, leaving them open and their hands hovering, ready to dip into jackets for weapons and firearms.

Another man, one of the Irish, opened his mouth to say something but twas cut off by a look from the Sicilian who'd made the bid. The Irishman's companions, one on each side, placed their hand on his arms. The Irish mobster slowly sat back down, glaring at the Sicilian in defiance.

"Sold!" the auctioneer declared, slamming his mallet down on the podium.

"Good," Joan grabbed the corners of the velvet cloth the artifact rested on and brought them up. She turned towards the winning bidder and said, "I'll meet you at your vehicle."

Joan drew the four corners together, slid a hand downward, tightening the makeshift bag, and wrapped a leather cord around the extra material protruding from the top.

The mercenary woman turned and strode off stage; parting the heavy curtains with one hand and carrying the velvet bag in the other. Hank saw the white light of an open door leading into a hallway beyond the curtain before it dropped closed.

Hank stood up, pulling away from Charles.

"Hey," Charles plucked at her silver-grey sleeve, "where are you going?"

"Oh, nowhere," Hank said, distracted, and stepped forward. She realized Charles wasn't letting go of her sleeve and stopped. "I just want to see that one more time before it leaves the building."

Hank brushed at the man's hand to get him to let go as she craned her neck towards the last place she saw Joan and the lamp.

"You don't have to chase after some woman to see anything," Charles stood and grabbed her hand and pulled it under his own arm and into the crook of his elbow. "I can let you see it all you want."

Hank looked down at their interlinked arms, then up at the man's face, realizing he was still here.

"What are you talking about?" Hank turned back towards the artifact.

"I just bought it," Charles's tone was smug and

suggestive, "and I can give you all the time you'd like with that magical genie's lamp, if you just give me some time with you."

Hank stopped craning her head and searching. She raised her chin, looking straight ahead, then slowly turned to look at the man, raising her face to meet his eyes.

"Are you saying," a sly smile spread across Hank's face, "that if I show you my treasures, you'll show me yours?"

Charles smiled and opened his mouth to reply, and Hank pulled pepper spray from her fanny pack with her free hand. She sprayed a direct stream, tracing a line across his eyes, up his nose, and into his open mouth. It reminded Hank of the old game at travelling carnivals where you sprayed the mouth of a plastic clown head with a water gun to inflate a balloon and win a prize.

The man's reply tuned into a gurgled scream of surprised pain. Charles's hands flew to his face and Hank pulled away. He stopped a hand-span from his burning features, screaming angry orders for someone to grab "that woman".

Hank ran forward, leapt on the stage, and rolled under the curtain. Getting to her feet, she ran to the open doorway.

Other voices muddled Charles's voice—some concerned, some mocking—as he commanded others to follow her and bring her back to him.

Chapter 16

Hank ran through the door and into the hall, making directional decisions without hesitating. Nothing about her showed panic. She focused on what needed done, withdrawing into herself. Her brain became like a computer, calculating everything from the timing of jumping over obstacles to her opponent's moves, all planned five steps ahead. She knew what people would do before they did.

Centering herself and her thoughts, she mentally dove into her current situation, and created a mental barrier to keep distractions out. She knew being too focused could be dangerous. In an out of sight, out of mind sort of situation if she left anything out of her calculations, it could throw a wrench in the works. She could end up with blinders on, and never see something coming.

Okay, she thought, *I don't know the layout of the building, but I know they modernized it. They incorporated and arranged the current floor plan over the over two-thousand-year-old ancient layout. This allowed for a lot of...*

The word slipped from her head as she turned a corner and saw a situation that was exactly the sort she'd been thinking about.

A small alcove built as the entryway to the bathrooms was ahead of her—a single unisex room (unlike bathrooms at the turn of the century) with a dozen enclosed stalls.

This would've made little sense in the ancient layout, she thought, *bathrooms usually had a long trough with a well pump at one end that trickled water along it. Considering the Greeks invented the ancestor of modern plumbing, this century's architects did a fair job of considering such things when they designed the facilities…in every way except where they placed them.*

Shaking away the distracting thoughts, Hank sidled around the built-in vestibule, her mind racing ahead of her.

Where would Joan be going? The woman needed to get the lamp out of here, and to…

Hank's mind jumped.

Was Charles a Russo? Was the man-boy who thought he was cleverly and effortlessly seducing me, the heir-apparent of the Sicilian mob?

Focus on one thing at a time, Hank thought. *First Joan and the lamp. Once that's taken care of, then the Russo boy won't be more than an afterthought. But if she gets away, then dealing with Charles might be necessary.*

She turned another corner, stepping aside for a trolley of rattling dishes and smiled at the porter steering it.

I won't be able to go back to what was, she continued. *That romantic, dangerous flirting I'd been leading him on with five minutes ago is gone. If I try a romantic track again…I know his type and he'd have to dominate me to the point of borderline abuse. And I don't take kindly to that kind of treatment with anyone, let alone to myself. I probably couldn't beat him down physically—though maybe I could with a little preparation time—but I know, without a doubt, I can beat him mentally.*

That boy is simple when it comes to social skills. He's a spoiled brat who expects everyone to kowtow to him. Well, this showed well enough in the short time that I interacted with him.

Joan's a different story, though, Hank sighed, turning another corner. *She's creative, inventive, and enjoys a challenge. In fact, she's driven by confrontation and crises. It's her drug of choice. Some adrenaline junkies like skydiving or parkour, but not Joan. She doesn't want a static challenge that you can stare at and take it in your own time. She wants something that actively fights back. She's like that in everything, even relationships, and it's a constant battle with her. She thrives on conflict.*

Joan has the lamp, is trying to remove it from the building, and deliver it to the Sicilians. Or at least to their courier. She'd head as directly as possible to where she needs to be to make this happen. Joan's never subtle on purpose.

Hank entered the main chamber where the party was still ongoing and glimpsed her opponent across the crowded floor. Joan brushed past a couple, the man smiling and speaking to her with his hand extended in greeting. His face fell as she pushed past, not even looking up at him.

The woman the man is with is probably his wife, she's older so probably not a mistress, Hank thought. *She's glaring at Joan, and her face is pruning and puckering in bitter disapproval. Definitely a wife, because a mistress would never worry about another woman walking away from the man she was with, but a wife would want him to network with important people. She's offended on his behalf because of the snubbing Joan just so bluntly gave him.*

Hank pushed into the crowd, weaving her way through the throng of people. She kept an eye on Joan, who moved at a brisk pace, but not so fast as to draw attention.

A familiar gait and body pattern caught Hank's eye. She didn't so much see him, as subconsciously recognize the way he moved and carried himself. Silver walked onto the large open floor, exiting a back hallway, and glancing over his shoulder.

The crowd was just beginning to notice the silent, but flashing, alarm. The red and white LED lights were much higher in this room, which had ten-meter ceilings, and was two-stories tall in this room with the balcony circling the second floor. The crowd milled about, drinks in hand, not wanting to leave and lose their place in the hall if it wasn't a genuine emergency.

"If it were important that we leave, someone in charge would make an announcement," a man in the crowd said in a loud voice.

Murmured agreements accompanied nods. The idea rode a tide of conversation across the room on a wave of repetition as people repeated the idea as if it were their own.

Silver noticed Hank and gave her a curt nod.

He slid through the crowd; Hank slowed for a moment, giving him part of her attention while still watching Joan nearing the edge of the room.

Silver moved like a dangerous animal. He was sinewy and lithe, a graceful dancer that never smiled or even glared. He had a grim and determined look of a man with a shovel in his hand and a long trench to dig if he wanted to survive whatever was coming.

He didn't get pleasure from a fight; he attained a goal. Unlike Joan, it wasn't the challenge that he craved, but rather, he faced challenges to gain something he wanted. He didn't seek conflict and went around it when possible.

But if it was inevitable, he squared his shoulders, set his feet, and put his back into it. He was a reed and bent with the wind, but when wielded as a weapon, he got to the point and left welts.

Hank gestured towards Joan, and Silver looked that way. Turning back to Hank, he nodded and adjusted his course towards the fleeing woman.

Making their way through the room, Hank and Silver glanced at one another, checking the other's course and pacing. They both stopped and pointed at one another simultaneously. From ten meters away, they mimed each other's actions and reactions without meaning to, looking like a fun-house mirror that altered reality.

They both pointed again, and at the same time they realized that the other was pointing at something past themselves. Both turned to look.

Hank saw a half dozen Italian men coming up behind her, three of them from the auction room. They stared directly at her, their shoulders hunched, and chins dropped, trying to do that looming, threatening presence thing that men used to intimidate. They stalked forward, the lead men shoving people roughly to the side, and the back ones keeping their hands under their designer suit jackets.

Silver saw a half dozen house security coming towards him. They wore the standard black pants, grey shirts with a pocket on each side of the chest, a thick shiny belt with hard leather pouches on it, and severe military haircuts. But these men didn't have the standard security issue deterrents. They each held an automatic pistol with digital sighting. Above them, on the second-floor balcony, was the mole-man, tall man, and good ol' broke-nose. The three pointed and spoke into their watches, giving directions to the men below. Mole-man looked confused and turned questioningly to the tall man.

Silver and Hank turned to look at one another and saw more movement as several groups of men pushed out from a hall and into the crowd.

Hank and Silver moved towards one another, even while following Joan's path.

"See the rough-looking men?" Hank asked when they were close enough to speak without being overheard.

"Which ones?" Hank saw Silver's hands twitch, as if he wanted to draw weapons, but he had none. "We got the house goons following me, the goomba goons following you, and then the guys who look like Yamaguchi-gumi, and then the disco boys, the oil barons, the political rally guys, and then the tropical island mob."

"The last ones," Hank gestured as she spoke, "Goombas are the Sicilians. They won the auction and Joan is bringing them the Jazeer's Light. The disco boys are the Irish mob, the oil barons are Saudis, the island boys are apparently a South American mob alliance, the political boys are Yanks, and you got the Yamaguchi-gumi correct. They all want the lamp."

"So," Silver said, turning to continue following Joan who'd disappeared into another hallway, "we're following Joan. The Sicilians, who she's supposed to be delivering the artifact to, are following you. Morgan's guys are following me, and everyone else is kinda following us, but only to go through us and get to Joan, who we're following. That about right?"

"Yeah," Hank said in a breath of air, "you've got it all covered."

"This is another fine pickle you've gotten us into, Stanley."

"The line is," Hank corrected, picking up the pace, "'Well, here's another nice mess you've gotten me into.' And it was Stan, not Stanley."

They'd almost reached the hallway when the

gunfire erupted, and the crowd panicked and stampeded.

Chapter 17

Silver spun to the left, moving behind a pillar twice as wide as his shoulders.

Hank dove to the right and behind a table with ice sculptures bracketing the pile of gifts and donation envelopes.

The groups of men met in the center of the floor; the security with their auto pistols and machismo, and the various mobsters with their club-like hands and lots of chutzpah.

They hadn't noticed each other, instead watching their quarry, Silver or Smith. Even mole-man, tall guy, and broke-nose only had eyes for Silver, not noticing the other interested parties enter the large room.

But once they met in the center, it was like thunder that starts low and slow, rumbling and building to a crescendo of sound with a boom that you can feel shake you.

The Irish disco boys, seeing the men with the weapons, reacted first. Crouching like feral cats in an alley, they let out a high-pitched whoop—again, not so different from cats in an alley—and leapt forward, colliding with the security officers.

One gun was pushed upward, and the guard's finger twitched on the trigger. A line of bullet holes shattered the ceiling fresco of Greek gods and monsters. The minotaur took a shot to the head, though Theseus was narrowly missed. Colored plaster rained down on the crowd.

The Americans took three large steps back, bumping into, knocking over, and stumbling into the people behind them.

The Saudi Arabians moved sideways, put their backs to a wall, and watched the situation with caution.

The Sicilians moved shoulder to shoulder, like a phalanx of Roman soldiers. As one, they crossed the room, making a beeline for Hank and Joan beyond her.

The Latin Americans turned on one another, seeing an opportunity to take out important men of rival groups in the confusion. Disrupting their private battle, the Yamaguchi-gumi joined in, hoping to take all of them out.

"I wish I'd thought of that," Silver shouted across to Hank, pointing at the fray. "It would've been an awesome plan!"

"You can appreciate your lack of creative planning later," Hank pulled into a crouch, looking towards the hall Joan disappeared down and then back to the approaching mobsters, "right now, we have a priceless artifact to save from its rightful owners."

Silver met her eyes as their individual gazes traversed from one problem and then back to the other.

He nodded.

"Lead the way," he bent and set his legs for a running start, "I've got your back."

Duck walking backwards, Hank tucked her back and shoulders under the heavily weighed down table, placed her hands on the underside, and stood up. Using her legs, she upset the table. Envelopes and boxes tumbled, sliding across the floor. The ice sculptures teetered, then toppled onto the floor, shattering into a thousand frozen crystalline gemstones being washed along by the water in the drainage tray underneath.

Silver reached behind him, grabbing the closest thing he could throw.

The potted frond plant flew across the space between Silver and the Sicilians, the heavy ceramic container it nested in leading the way. The earthenware container hit the lead man in the gut, knocking him back, and he fell to the floor. The pot shattered, scattering shards of pottery and dark, rich potting soil throughout the water and ice of the broken sculptures.

The Sicilians lost traction and their footing, slipping along the floor and colliding into one another and other panicked guests.

The ice, water, and soil quickly blended into mud under the feet of dozens of people running in random directions.

Most folks sought escape while others started filming on their cardphones, small electromagnetic drones the size of a business cards humming into the air to get a birdseye view of the chaos. Some tried to assist the security guards subdue the mobsters.

One man scurried around on hands and knees scooping up donation envelopes, stuffing them into his jacket pockets, which he'd pulled up over his head to make it harder for the constant camera surveillance in this day and age to recognize and track him.

Hank turned and jogged for the hall. She knew she couldn't go too fast. That would cause her to be careless and miss important details, like an ambush.

I only have so much perception to go around, she thought, *and need to assign it astutely, which in my mind, perception should always be astute by definition. If I had to divide up a hundred percent of my awareness, then only about thirty percent can go to running, which includes finding the best path, avoiding obstacles, and so on. Twenty percent for thinking ahead, second guessing others, and predicting what's around corners. Ten percent focused on my body and well-being, hydration, breathing, exhaustion, knee or foot pain, and so on.*

She dodged around an older couple holding onto one another, trying not to slip on the mud slick.

That leaves forty percent for focusing on my direct quarry. Except it isn't a full forty percent, is it? Because each time I split my attention, my focus, it takes a small percentage to shift gears between focuses, and bridge the gap between things I'm thinking about, and my actions and reactions.

She was almost to the exit Joan had run through.

It's that way for anything, which is why you can mess up your craft project when watching TV, or wreck your car when texting, and so on. I figure it takes maybe two percent each time I split my attention, but it increases exponentially each time. So, thirty, then two percent to split, twenty more, then four percent to split again, ten more, and eight to split again, twenty for planning, and sixteen more to split the fourth time, and then forty for the quarry.

That couldn't be right, she thought, sprinting for the hall, *that would put me at one hundred and fifty percent, plus the extra split for doing this math.*

She entered the hallway, stumbling over a taped down power cord at the edge of the room.

See, she thought, *that's what I meant about splitting your attention, and you should stop doing all this puerile math now and focus on the task at hand, silly girl. What would Silver think? I bet he saw you trip.*

With that, she emptied her head of all the extraneous thoughts, and hyper-focused on her goal.

Silver was a dozen meters behind her and had seen her misstep.

Who used wired cords anymore? The thought niggled at Silver, *Especially since power storage had taken leaps and bounds with graphene, and miniaturization keeping pace?*

He followed Hank deeper into the hall, head pivoting left and right, and his hearing focused on pursuit from behind.

They laid on the speed, bouncing off walls, and skidding around corners.

"I see her," Hank exclaimed, breathless, "just ahead, around the next corner."

They ran all out and recklessly. After a few more turns they burst out into a green courtyard, a helicopter sitting in the middle. The rotors picked up speed.

Joan had one foot inside the rear compartment, gripping the exterior handhold.

As the helicopter rose, she looked over her shoulder at Hank. Their eyes met, and Joan grinned, jiggling the makeshift velvet bag. She passed it to someone in the vehicle and pulled herself inside.

Leaning out, Joan raised a one-finger salute to her pursuers, accompanied by a big smile.

By the time Hank reached the helipad, the bird was thirty meters up and banking left and rising fast.

It zoomed off to the southwest as Silver stumbled to a stop beside Hank. The two exchanged glances, too winded to do more than that.

The ground rumbled.

Hank and Silver turned to see orange flames explode skyward from the center of the building. Thick, greasy, black smoke followed, erupting up and outward, flowing down the building.

People poured out of every side of the building.

A second explosion knocked most of them to the ground, rocking Hank and Silver back on their heels.

"Someone," Silver panted out a question, "wanted to eliminate the competition?"

"Joan," Hank bent over, her hands on her knees, her upper body heaving, "and whoever she's working for?"

"Maybe," Silver stretched, his fists in the small of his back, "but whoever it was doesn't matter right this second. We should make ourselves scarce before someone decides to question everyone here."

Saman waited at the hangar housing Silver's plane when the taxi dropped them off. He wore almost identical clothes to the last time they'd seen him, except a black suede suit jacket with the sleeves pulled up covered his tight shirt, and his five-o'clock shadow was a definitive goatee.

His handful of thugs were also at the hanger—the two from Silver's warehouse giving a small wave—though the rest could have been different men and women. They were the type of lackeys that comic book villains and government agencies picked up at the hireling store and didn't differ much in appearance.

"I am guessing you didn't get the lamp," the man smiled a tight, sympathetic smile, tinged with frustration.

Saman smelled of pungent, exotic spices mixed with the aroma of grease and fuel in an odd, but not unattractive, way. He stepped forward to shake each of their hands.

"You do know we don't work for you, right?" Silver said, shaking the man's hand, staring him straight in the eye.

Saman's smile changed, becoming a wider and more honest grin, teeth peeking out from between his lips.

Hank shook Saman's hand without comment but watched him with a funny look on her face.

Silver watched the exchange between the two closely.

"Of course, you do not," Saman's face changed again, and he humbly dropped his eyes, "I did not mean to seem forward. I only want to see your success and this artifact of my past, my land, and my people safely delivered to where it belongs."

"Is that why you're here?" Silver clicked the pay app and waved the taxi away.

"Yes," Saman smiled widely, his white teeth brilliant against his beige skin, "and to see if I can offer you assistance in your upcoming trip to Sicily."

"Sicily?" Silver stopped and stiffly turned back to Saman. "What makes you think we're going there?"

"The sale to the Russo's was recorded instantly after the auction," Saman explained, waving away the question, "and considering it is still a stolen item, I believe I can safely assume that the two of you will continue in your pursuit."

"Of course," Silver said, his posture unchanging.

They stood in awkward silence, seconds ticking by, with the hired guards of Saman looking anywhere except at the three of them.

"Yeah," Hank broke the tension, "there is something you can do for us."

"Anything," Saman smiled again, spreading his hands in front of him, "tell me and it shall be done."

Hank smiled back, a tight smile. Her brow furrowed as she studied the man.

"You can," she hesitated, "contact the museum board for us, and ask that they be waiting at the airport in—where did we figure out the Russos are based?"

Hank turned to Silver.

"Catania," Silver and Saman answered in unison.

Silver and Hank turned to Saman.

"I also have done my homework, as you say in the west," Saman innocently raised his eyebrows, "and I know where a family with as much influence as the Russos maintain their seat of power."

"Seat of power," Silver said slowly, rolling the words over his tongue like a well-aged wine. "An interesting way to phrase it."

The two of them slumped in the leather seats of Silver's private jet as it taxied down the runway.

"Don't ever make me do something like that again," Hank pressed a cold-water bottle to her forehead.

"I don't think anyone could make you do anything you don't choose to do," Silver smiled, "but which thing in particular do you mean?"

"The flirting to get in," Hank paused, then shuddered, "especially with a degenerate likes Charles Russo."

Hank did some research in the cab and had been correct about Charles. He was first in line to take control of the Russo family when his father passed or stepped down, whichever came first.

"I didn't make you do that." Silver leaned back in his seat, closing his eyes. "You chose to do that. It wasn't even remotely my idea. I would've used my money to buy my way in. Besides, Charles is probably dead now."

"He might be." Hank sighed, twisting open the lid of the bottle and taking a deep drink, "But I hope not."

"Really?" Silver cracked one eye open and turned his head slightly to look at Hank.

"Really," Hank held the bottle up to the light, looking through it at nothing in particular, "the man is a chauvinistic, egotistical, spoiled brat. But that isn't a death sentence."

"Fair enough." Silver closed his eyes again.

The cabin fell silent as they gained altitude except for the high-pitched whine of the engines, their ears filling with pressure.

Hank needs a distraction, Silver decided, *or else she'll mentally beat herself up for what happened back there.*

"Catania next," Silver said, "but where after that? Have you mapped a route?"

"Oh, yes," Hank's voice took on a mildly excited tone, eager to change the subject, "just let me pull it up and I'll pop it up on the screen."

She fiddled with her cardphone, linking it to the plane's FiSys. A map of Greece appeared on the screen, panning out, a red dot over Thessaloniki.

"We'll leave Greece," Hank explained, a red line appearing, "cross the Ionian Sea to Sicily, and the city of Catania…"

The line met another red dot off the coast of Italy, on the island of Sicily, highlighting their destination. The screen zoomed in, showing streets and buildings, the red line marking their path on arrival.

Travis I. Sivart

Chapter 18

"Catania is a beautiful city," Hank explained through the earpiece. "Almost three-thousand years of culture and history has given the Sicilian island layers, figuratively and literally. Oceanfront to the east, overlooking the Ionian Sea. The coast of mainland Italy is just over seventy kilometers away and hidden below the northeastern horizon. And look at the looming, cloud-shrouded peak of Mount Etna to the northwest. It's one of the most active volcanos in Europe. The glow of the volcano is often a beacon in the night or causes an eerie glow in early morning fogs.

"The city is layered, too, as you saw," she continued. "I love how the architecture ranges from the dull yellows and beiges with square, squat buildings of a simpler era, to the domes and spires of the Baroque period with its wrought iron streetlights and railings, to the bright oranges and reds of long buildings of the tourist areas along the coastline."

She sighed in Silver's ear.

"It's easy to wander through an ancient weed-broken amphitheater, to the business district of cars and suits, into a church with frescos and stained-glass honoring Sant'Agata. Then go outside again and past the resting place of the magical and mythical mascot of the city—the Fontana dell'Elefante, also known as Fountain of the Elephant—to grey, stone courtyards full of the sound and motion of pigeons and ending in the echoing alleys full of the sights and salt-tangy smells of the seafood markets. Outdoor cafes, awnings, and the hum of mopeds weave through all of it, tying these very different places and times into one unique and beautiful city that compares to no other."

Silver smiled, waiting in a covered alley, happy to be comfortable again. He wore his standard black with silver accents on the belts, pouches, weapons, gizmos, and tech distributed about his body.

"I don't know why I had to be here," Hank said into his earbud via their direct connect, "laying in the bushes, staring through a scope and recording their conversation while you lollygag at street corners watching the nightlife."

"You wanted to do it," Silver said dryly, scanning the crowd, "insisted on doing it. You accused me of saying you weren't up to the task when I said I'd do it."

Hank adjusted her boonie hat, pulling the brim down and to one side to block out the overhead lights whose glare interfered with her surveillance. She tugged at the olive-drab, double-breasted canvas peacoat, pulling it back under her hips where it had pulled up, adjusting her positioning.

She lined her eye up with the scope again, her shoulder tight against the stock as she looked across the kilometer and a half of hillsides and into the Russo compound window.

"Charles is in the office, looking petulant, and arguing with his father, Robert." She gave a play by play to Silver. "The senior Russo is a salt-and-pepper bearded, rotund man with an easy confidence. He doesn't seem to be angry or be raising his voice. Instead, he has a superior manner. Maybe that comes with age and experience, but whatever it is, it allows him to intimidate someone while he maintains a smile and laughs from what I can see."

She stopped talking, and Silver heard her adjust her position.

"Hold on," Hank's voice was muffled as she pressed her cheek to the stock of her weapon and twisted for a better look, "I think they're done arguing now. Someone else is coming into the room. The butler is gesturing; I can't see who's coming in, but it's a man in an expensive suit. A white suit, and he has light hair. Oh. Oh my. You won't believe this."

Silence fell over the comm. Silver waited, thrusting his head forward and tilting it slightly, his eyebrows rising, showing his expectation even though Hank had no way to see this.

Silver and Hank had reconnoitered the compound extensively over the past week, checking satellite photographs, city records, and other less common methods. They'd gathered information without drawing attention. They'd set up scripted meetings with various employees of the Russos, all which felt like very incidental and spontaneous encounters to the people they'd questioned.

It wasn't easy to do in regard to a family that was constantly under public scrutiny, but it wasn't impossible, either. The bounty hunter and the archeologist were both very good at their specific types of research and complemented each other's skill sets.

And now, Hank lay on her belly under a bush, watching the sprawling house through the scope on her weapon, while Silver leaned against a wall in an alley, talking to her, his foot resting on a sleek, low Bodyzoom.

The Bodyzoom was how he'd get there if needed. It was an enclosed, motorized body board that could top speeds of one-hundred and fifty kilometers per hour in normal circumstances, and three-hundred and twenty kilometers per hour on a perfectly smooth surface with no curves. It didn't have wheels, but was a hover board, using magnetic technology that floated it about fifteen centimeters off the ground. It could even hit eighty kilometers per hour across smooth waters.

The device was one of the many inventions and investments Silver created to support his income, and it had made him quite a bit of money. It also made him enemies. When he'd released it to the public, it caused companies to crumble and fall as their own versions were beat to the market. Silver's was more durable and even gained a military contract. That made a couple of people pretty upset with Silver.

"It's Roberts," Hank's voice was a whisper in Silver's ear.

"What is?" Silver asked, pulled from his reverie.

"Roberts," Hank breathed, and Silver could hear her squirming, "Aaron Roberts just walked into the room."

"Why would he be there?"

"Hush, I'm turning up the sound," Hank shushed Silver. "I'll patch you through."

The sound on the earbud popped, a warm buzz that hinted at the technology breaking into an eavesdropping-proof room. Rooms or structures often had a metal cage built into the walls, similar to chicken wire, which they could run electric pulses through to create a warm hum and block distance listening devices.

Hank had gotten around this by sending a box of cigars with a signal puller hidden in it, causing the sound-blocking pulse to instead draw to it and allow eavesdropping the old-fashioned way.

"Bob," Aaron Roberts moved across the room to embrace the heavy man as Hank watched through her scope, "it's good to see you."

"It's good to see you, too, my old friend." The senior Russo's voice had the sound of sand sliding across metal, smooth with a hint of a scrape, and the undertone of joy and laughter.

"I hear your boy," Aaron gestured towards Charles, who stood staring out one of the four floor-to-ceiling windows with his arms crossed, "successfully purchased and retrieved my artifact from that swindler Ambrose?"

"Not quite," Russo laughed, "that delightful and sexy merc of yours, Joan, deserves more credit for that accomplishment than my son."

"Oh, really?" Aaron looked around. "And where is she? Will she be joining us to celebrate this union of families and merger of companies?"

"Yes," Russo said slowly, "but she's rounding up our final guests first."

"Oh?" Aaron moved to the silver cart in front of the window, lifting a carafe and pouring a glass of wine. "And where are they hiding?"

Hank watched Russo move behind Aaron, close one eye like he was trying to see something in the distance, raise an arm above the taller man's shoulder, and point in her direction.

"She should be right about there," Russo said, and Aaron looked down the length of the man's hairy arm, "at least according to our triangulation of her listening signal."

"Oh, yes," Aaron said, raising a glass in Hank's

direction. "I see Joan standing over someone hidden in a bush. Do you think she'll shoot her?"

Silver heard a rustling noise like fingers on the mic that fed sound to his earbud.

"Come and get her," Joan's voice hissed into Silver's ear.

The line went dead.

The Bodyzoom zipped through traffic. Silver lay on his belly, the plastic shell over him, and steering with his legs splayed like a frog's, each on their own platform. Shifting his weight and pulling his legs up or straightening them controlled the direction of the personal vehicle.

The machine smoothly mounted the sidewalk, then glided back into traffic, sliding to the center of the road between two lanes of vehicles, and then cut across one lane, zipped forward, and back to the center line again, gaining another car's length.

He'd considered using a flying version but thought that might attract too much attention. He wanted to beeline for the compound, but this version of the Bodyzoom was low and sleek and built for speed on the roads. It didn't hover high enough to handle off-road action.

The estate was about six kilometers west of Catania, and Silver knew he'd be there in a couple of minutes. He'd left the city limits and crested the hill where the walled estate should come into sight.

He caught air coming over the hill, and the view opened underneath him. A blue electrical haze encompassed Silver and his vehicle. Since he didn't build this model for being over thirty centimeters off the ground, Silver was unable to avoid the trap as he sailed more than a meter above the road.

The Bodyzoom lost power; the front dipping as gravity took over, and Silver hit the ground nose first at ninety kilometers per hour. The vehicle flipped and cartwheeled sideways down the road.

Safety features triggered, exploding into action. Protective foam, airbags, and tension restraints worked in tandem to protect the passenger, but it wasn't enough to help Silver.

Everything went black.

Chapter 19

Silver woke in a cell, of sorts. The room, partially completed, had fitted-stone walls. Vertical wooden supports, some with insulation in between, was half-completed with drywall. A damp and musty smell lingered, blending with the dust of dried spackling mud and sanded wallboards. A semi-circular, sepia-colored stain spread across some indicating a water leak.

Small rectangular windows lined the upper part of the wall to Silver's left. A small person could squeeze through one, he noted, but they didn't look like they opened and had bars.

To his right was a cell door with vertical metal bars spattered with lichen-like rust patches. Horizontal bars intersected at knee and chest height.

Silver wiggled. Thick leather straps lined with sheep's wool wrapped around his wrist, ankles, thighs, waist, and neck. Someone had strapped him to what felt like a repurposed medical bed.

He tested the restraints, straining upward. He coughed as the straps bit into him.

"Silver?" called a female voice with an Irish lilt. "Is that you?"

"You can recognize me by my cough?" His voice broke and sounded strained.

Parched, he ran his tongue over his dry and cracked lips. Laying on his back caused him to breathe through his mouth.

"Yes," Hank answered, sounding exasperated, "I

am sooo enthralled with your annoying dulcet tones that I've memorized your very breath and pacing of speech."

Silver's head throbbed, the words rolling through his confused thoughts. He grunted and made an extended muddled noise.

"I see," Hank's voice was close, but rebounded oddly, "think about it, Silver, who else would be in a recently refurbished and redecorated medieval dungeon with me? I wonder when they'll be installing the muzak to help with the psychological torture of their current guests."

"Okay, okay," Silver stared at the ceiling. "I get it. Calm down."

"Oh, that's a wonderful suggestion after I thought you were dead for the last eighteen hours, Silver." Hank's sarcasm pitched to a new level of biting. "Telling someone to calm down always does just exactly that. Those words are known to soothe and bring someone to a perfect Zen-like state."

"Look," anger cut through Silver's exhaustion, "I just woke up after being in a crash on my Bodyzoom at almost ninety kilometers per hour. It threw me head over heels for about fifty meters and did a series of cartwheels before I passed out, and god knows what after the g-forces and impacts caused me to black out. And I did all that while rushing to the Russo compound to help you, since it sure sounded like you were in trouble. So, if you have some more caustic wit to bestow upon me, do it now before I get out of these restraints and have my hands free to answer you with!"

Silver panted with the effort of his outburst and pushing against his restraints.

The room fell quiet except for his breathing.

"Boy," Hank muttered, "you sure do wake up cranky. And this means you've probably lost all your stuff again, doesn't it? I'm beginning to think you just like being naked."

"Damn it, Hank, I'm not naked!" Silver laughed, a ragged noise punctuated by coughing.

Hank's muffled laugh joined Silver's, and he knew she was covering her mouth self-consciously.

After a few minutes of silence, Hank spoke again.

"So," she said, "do you have a plan, or are you too tired after your little tumble to think one up?"

"Of course, I have a plan." Silver sighed. "I just need a few minutes to think of it. Are you tied down, too?"

Hank's voice was close, but he didn't think it was in a cell next to his.

"No? No," Hank's voice was slow, and Silver wondered if it was concern or worry he heard. "Did they tie you down?"

"Yeah, they did. Cuffs, belts, restraints, the whole nine yards. I can't even lift my head to look around. What's this place like?"

"Why would they tie you down, but not me?" The ire rose in Hank's voice again, her accent thickening.

"Let's thank them for that, Hank, and try not to give them any reason to change their minds. It'll be easier to get out of this mess if we aren't both strapped to a table."

"Well," Hank huffed, "yeah, okay."

"So, where are we?"

"We're in a…" Hank hesitated, "in a basement. I think the original construction might be seventeenth century, and they're redoing it. They're covering some beautiful examples of the architecture of the period.

They really knew how to build things; these could literally be the building blocks and foundation of the renaissance we're imprisoned within."

"Hank," Silver noted the dreamy quality coming into the woman's voice and interrupted to bring her back on track, "describe the actual rooms, not the history and technique of how they designed and built the place. Please."

"Oh, right, sorry about that." Hank breathed in, and Silver could almost see her scrunching up her face to focus on the task at hand. "It looks like there are six cells, or rooms. Each one has a heavy but rusted door made of bars. Most look to be dry walled over, and they've installed electric in the hall, but not in the cells."

The sound of metal-on-metal cut through the conversation, and Hank and Silver fell silent. A deep, grinding rasp echoed around them, suggesting a heavy door with years of rust build up. A whistled tune accompanied by crisp, clipped footfalls approached. The groaning and hollow boom of the heavy door drowned it out for a moment.

Aaron Roberts came into Silver's limited view. The man's short cropped white hair was perfect and glittered in the overhead LED lighting. He wore his usual white suit jacket and pants with unblemished and polished black shoes and belt. Even his jewelry matched the motif, sporting white gold with onyx highlights on his ring, cufflinks, and watch face.

The man stopped, turned towards Silver, and smiled his crooked smile. Roberts paused for a moment, studying the bound man, and then looked back and to his right, towards Hank. He wore an arrogant smile when he turned back.

"Hey, man," Silver said, raising his chin slightly in

greeting, "I'm good, nothing broken. You can let me up from this bed now."

"Oh," Roberts frowned and shook his head, "you should never attempt to be clever, Mr. Silver. It isn't your strong suit. But I don't think that'll be an issue for you much longer."

"I don't get it," Hank pressed to the bars of her cell, her face wedged between so she could see the man, "you hired us. Why are we here, and you out there?"

"Mz. Smith," Roberts said haughtily, "you are here because you're young, naïve, arrogant, and have something that you need to prove so badly that you ignore all common sense. Mr. Silver is here because I had a plan."

"You come on over here, ya rich bastard," Hank crooked a finger in Roberts's direction, "and I'll give you a wee bit of my common sense."

"Shhh, girl," Roberts waved a hand at her dismissively, "the adults are talking. Besides, don't you want to hear why Silver is going to die? If you're really good, maybe I'll leave you alive to tell other folks the cautionary tale. Of course, you'll be doing it from prison for all your heinous crimes."

"I haven't done anything wrong," Hank spat, "and who the hell says, 'heinous crimes' anymore?"

"Doesn't matter, does it?" Roberts turned and walked in front Hank. "I have footage of you involved in a firefight in downtown London, and picture and video of you at a Greek auction attacking the man who just legally purchased a priceless artifact, and then I have the police report of how you were found under a bush with a high-powered rifle pointing at one of Catania's most respected citizens."

Hank stared at Roberts, sputtering, spittle flying from her lips.

"Now, as for your friend here," Roberts strolled back to Silver's cell, his hands in his pockets, "I don't know if he'll even make it to prison. You see, Mz. Smith, Silver and I go way back, though we've never met."

Silver stared at the ceiling, listening, his muscles twitching.

"I first learned of Silver, and his company Jones Industries, when he began producing graphene. Such a simple product, it never really gained any attention. Just like the name of his company, Jones Industries." Roberts laughed, his tone sardonic, and rocked back on his heels slightly. "No one noticed it. It was small and with a name like Jones, no one bothered to look at it twice. It was like it wasn't even trying to get noticed, though it was publicly traded.

"His small company cornered the next big revolution in technology, making solar panels and electric car power sources to begin with, and computers, cardphones, interface technologies like the contact lenses linked to cardphones or weapons, and then even moving into bullet-proof vests and other things. Hell, the opportunities for graphene are endless.

"Then there were the magnetic propulsion systems. The uses for those were limitless, especially when blended with the energy storing and producing capabilities of graphene. And now we have hover everything. Even the Bodyzoom. I was in a production race with you over that and you beat me out, causing me to lose billions of dollars when yours came out first, with more options than mine.

"I tried to get a piece of that pie, by hook or by crook. I tried to get contracts, I inserted spies into his company, I undercut his prices on similar products, but each and every time I did something, Jones Industries countered it. And you know what the worst part was?"

"You hate Silver because of money?" Hank asked. "That's a bit sad, isn't it?"

Roberts was pacing now, not even seeming to notice he was doing it.

"He and his company didn't even notice me and my company. They weren't putting any effort to block me, they just did it as if I were inconsequential. So, I researched them, or the company at least. Silver was like a ghost, and it took effort to find out exactly who Augustus Jones was, and why he never appeared in the public view."

"Augustus?" Hank said, the sound of her voice betraying her smirk.

Roberts ignored her and continued his tirade.

"But I did find out." Roberts stood outside of Silver's cell now, staring in, his shoulders hunched.

From what Silver could see from the corner of his eye, Roberts looked like an albino vulture watching his next meal, and waiting for it to die so he could devour it.

"Even when I figured out who ran Jones Industries, and that he moonlighted as a bounty hunter with some defunct moral code, I had a hard time tracking him down.

"In the meantime, he and his company continued to beat me in every way. Until Joan Williams came to me to sell a certain Chinese artifact and mentioned the man in black and silver.

"It got a lot easier then," Roberts chuckled, "and

I set out some bait. A certain younger woman. An independent and strong-willed woman who might remind Silver of someone he once knew, someone he once loved. His sister, Charlotte."

Silver flinched, his head jerking towards the man. The restraints creaked as Silver unconsciously strained against them.

Roberts giggled.

"Oh yes," Roberts wrapped his hands around the bars in front of him, still chuckling, "I know you, Silver. And I set up the perfect trap, a young woman who would rush headfirst into danger, and a priceless artifact."

Roberts stopped, as if coming to his senses, tilted his head, and smiled, cocky and self-assured.

"Oh, the Jazeer's Light is a special treasure. Did you know it's said that it can summon a genie? A real ifrit, an actual djinn, or djinni. Like the creature from Aladdin or One Thousand and One Arabian Nights. But I really wanted it for the reason I told you. So many people wanted it and I knew it would bring together the criminal underworld from across the globe.

"Every mob boss who possessed it has died, but before they did, they had incredible success. Even Russo made quite the profit by selling it to me, as well as securing business contracts that will make him and his family rich for decades to come.

"But now I have it," Roberts stood up, unwrapped his fingers from the bars and flexed them, "and I won't make the same mistakes they did. As you've seen, I do my research, and use knowledge to gain power.

"So," Roberts dusted at his suit, streaking it with red brown from the rust of the bars, leaving smears that looked like dried blood, "I'll leave you here for the authorities, and as targets of a half dozen mob bosses. I suspect that you're both already on more than one bounty hunter hit list.

"And without its leader, Jones Industries will wilt and fall apart, allowing me to pick it apart, buying it and dismantling it piece by piece. All in all, I think it'll be rather fulfilling work."

The ground rumbled, and the building shook. Small sprays of plaster and pebbles trickled down from the ceiling in a half dozen places.

Roberts looked around, his eyes settling on Silver.

A rain of powder from above Silver spotted his face, his dark skin blotching white and gray.

"Well," Roberts chuckled, "perhaps the criminals won't get you. Maybe a stone will fall from the ceiling and crush your skull instead. Either way, I have a helicopter waiting for me. I just wanted to say goodbye."

With that Roberts began whistling, turned, and walked towards the door, the heels of his shoes clicking out a rhythm to match the tune. He paused for a moment, looking down at the stains on his outfit, brushed at them, grunted, and began walking again, this time without the tune.

The door creaked open, and someone asked if everything was okay in Italian. They lost the rest as the portal boomed closed.

Chapter 20

Silver turned his head toward the wall, blinking dust from his eyes. Through the small window he could see the gathering dusk lit with an orangey-red glow.

The building shook again.

"I got nothing," Silver said.

"Oh, don't be silly," Hank said, her voice distant, "you still have your company, and your friends, and your life."

"No," Silver turned his head towards the cell door, "I have no plan. I really don't have any friends, either, just business associates, but that's neither here nor there."

"What?" Hank's voice was louder again, and the sound of lightweight metal scraping thick, heavy metal came from her direction. "I'm your friend, Silver. You'll be able to tell because I'm here for you, and you'll be able to tell in the future by the way I make fun of your real name."

"I don't make fun of your real name," Silver growled, but it had no strength behind it.

Silver was exhausted to the bone. Not just because of the accident, or lack of food or water since last night, but because the fight had gone out of him.

Because of me, Hank will die, he thought, *my company will fail, and thousands of people will be out of work, and they and their families will struggle because of that.*

"Fair point," Hank said, her voice straining. She grunted and took in a deep breath.

"What're you doing over there?" Silver looked at the ceiling again. "You sound constipated. Wait, do you have a toilet in your cell? I hadn't thought about it, but now that I am, I really need to pee."

The building shook again, and a loud thud came from outside Silver's cell.

Silver turned his head to squint at the hall through the haze cloud of plaster dust.

Hank stepped into his view, smiling, brushing plaster and rock dust from her hair and clothes, shaking her head.

Silver stared, his mouth open.

"How?" Silver croaked.

"It has to do with all that architecture stuff you didn't want to know about," Hank said airily, waving a dismissive hand, "and knowing how the cell was built. It's a simple matter of using a chair as a fulcrum to lift the cell door off its hinge pins. I just waited for another tremor, then popped it off. Maybe the guards heard it fall, but maybe they thought it was just damage from the earthquake."

"That's not an earthquake," Silver gestured towards the small window with a jerk of his head, "that's Mount Etna. She's erupting."

"Really?" Hank craned her neck to look. Seeing the red glow with the orange gout of lava and flame streak across the sky, she tightened her lips. "Well, I guess we're going to need to step this plan up."

Helpless and bound, Silver watched Hank drag a metal framed chair with an ugly orange pleather seat from the hall.

She wedged the front legs under the lower set of bars of the door, angling the chair backwards, using the rear legs as a fulcrum. She paused, waiting for something.

She drew in a quick breath and pushed her weight on the back of the chair, causing the cell door to pop upward just as the ground and building shook again.

Hank's feet came off the ground as she put all her weight on the back of the chair to lift the metal bars of Silver's door. Though the door went up, barely balanced above the hinge pins on the stone door frame, it didn't fall.

When she was in her own cell and had performed her escape trick, the door was positioned to fall outward, into the hall. It was the same for Silver's door, but she was on the opposite side, so the force she was applying pushed the door into the frame instead of out of it and towards the hall where it could freely tumble away.

"Son of a…" Hank muttered.

Keeping her body on the chair back, she leaned forward to grab the bars so she could pull them towards her and the hallway. The chair teetered forward, and the bars threatened to fall back onto its pins.

Hank wiggled further up onto the chair back, swinging one leg over it and pressed her hips onto the back of the chair to keep it from rocking forward and losing everything she'd accomplished so far.

Silver watched her, his leg twitching. He wanted to lash out to kick the door outward to help open up the room that confined him. But he couldn't move. He held his breath, and let it out slowly, making himself relax and wait, relying on the only person who could help him now.

He'd worked alone for a long time and wasn't used to relying on anyone to save him. It wasn't always that way. He'd even once had a protégé of sorts. Hank reminded Silver of that kid, but she was less temperamental. She still jumped once she made a decision and was quick to act without thinking at times, times that his experience told him that there was a better way. But she was less angry and had a better head on her shoulders.

Hank's fingers brushed the bars. She stretched further, curling the tips, the first knuckle, around the bars as the chair teetered back and forth. She wrapped her hands around it, rocking on the chair.

The tremor subsided to a barely a vibration. If she pulled the door down now, the guards outside the door would hear it, alerting them to the activity within the cells.

Hank knew she had to make her move. Silver was depending on her. She had to do it, no matter the consequences, and she knew she may not have another chance.

She pulled on the door. The chair rocked forward, and the cell door fell back into place on its pins.

Hank let out a squeak of frustration. The chair fell to all fours with a metallic thunk, jarring the woman, and she fell sideways to the floor.

Silver closed his eyes and turned his face back to the ceiling.

Hank stood, moving quickly, and jammed the chair back into place. Throwing herself onto the back of the chair again, she tried to wedge the chair back up, attempting to lift the door again.

"Hey!" came a voice to her left.

Turning her head, she saw a face framed in the small, barred window of the outer door. A guard, with wide eyes, stared at her.

She threw herself on to the makeshift lever again.

The entire room jumped and buckled with a stronger tremor, another stream of lava showing through the window across the room. The cell door bounced and slammed into the top of the door frame, and rebounded outward, falling towards Hank.

The outer door opened, framing three men with automatic weapons in the wide doorway. They brought the weapons up.

The cell door fell, and Hank rolled to her right, gunfire erupting around her. Loud pops accompanied sparks as bullets bounced on stone and iron. It was like being in the deadliest popcorn popper she could imagine, and the heat was only getting more intense.

Hank scrambled onto all fours and dove through the opening into Silver's cell.

The footfalls of the guards in the hall approached as they ran towards her.

She looked at Silver. He was smiling and gave her a small nod, then he focused on the hall.

Hank pressed herself against the wall just inside the cell, beside the doorway.

The tip of a weapon appeared in the entrance.

"Afternoon gentlemen," Silver's voice was still rough, but had a quality of charisma and confidence that hadn't been there the last time he spoke, "if you care to set me free, I can make it worth your while. If you don't, then it looks like you're in for a world of hurt."

Hank paused for a moment, watching the muzzle of the weapon. If it went down, there was a chance they'd be able to negotiate. If it didn't...

The firearm rose.

Hank's hands shot out, grabbing the barrel with

her left and flipping it down, her right hand gripping it underneath near the trigger guard to become a pivot point.

The gun flipped upside down, and Hank pushed it towards the hall. The guard's finger involuntarily pressed the trigger. A bark of gunfire went off, and the man did a silly little dance as a half dozen rounds entered his midsection.

Hank tore the weapon from his hands as he fell. She twirled it around and into a firing position. Dropping to the ground, she fired the weapon into the hallway with a back and forth strafing movement; the recoil causing the weapon fire to trace upwards.

The two remaining guards performed a jerky dance before crumbling to the ground, one with a handful of wounds in his hips and belly, the other showing injuries to his chest and head.

Hank took a moment before she stood. She looked over at the three men. The first, whose weapon she had taken, lay at her feet in a fetal position with his hands clutched to his midsection. He wept and choked.

The second had stumbled backwards into the wall behind him and slid down it. He held his belly and stared at her with wide and disbelieving eyes.

The third sprawled across the hall, part of his face missing, and his legs spasming.

Hank swallowed, realizing her last meal was debating on leaving her, and her throat spasmed.

She shut down her thoughts, didn't let herself think about what had just happened. Instead, she moved.

Bending, she drew a combat knife from the waist sheath of the first man. She stepped over him and kicked away the weapon of the second man propped against the wall. It slid towards the cell they'd imprisoned her in, scraping along the floor and rebounding off the wall three meters away.

Hank turned back, meaning to head for the table where Silver was tied down, but she stopped. Her eyes lingered on the dead and dying men, but her mind couldn't connect. It was like a car whose transmission was slipping and wouldn't fall into gear. Her brain revved, but wouldn't move forward, instead spinning in place and making a lot of white noise, unable to process what needed done.

"Hank," came a voice, "Henrietta, you need to look at me now."

Hank looked towards the sound. It was Silver. *Augustus,* she thought, and wondered why she felt she should smile or laugh at the name.

"That's it, Hank," Silver said.

His face came into focus, white plaster from the crumbling ceiling dusting his skin. His voice was harsh, but not from emotion. It was gentle in that way, coaxing and comforting. She felt like she should know why it was rough but couldn't put her finger on it right now.

"Bring the knife over here," Silver said, and she knew he'd been talking for a while now. Maybe a few seconds, but it could've been minutes. "Come over here and cut the straps."

She took a step towards him.

"That's it," he said, "come on over. We need to get out of here, but first we need to get me loose."

Hank moved towards him, seeing the knife in her hand and realizing what she'd meant to do with it.

She wiped at her wet face and set to freeing her friend.

She cut the restraint on his right hand.

"I'll take that now," Silver said, holding his hand out for the knife. "You just watch me to make sure I don't cut myself."

She handed him the knife.

Silver freed his waist, his right thigh, his chest, his neck, and then his left wrist. Sitting up, he cut the remaining straps away.

"Wait here." Silver took Hank by the shoulders and turned her towards the small window. "Watch the sky, we need to know what that volcano is doing. I'll be right back."

Hank watched the glowing sky as Silver slipped into the hallway.

Silver stepped over the man in the fetal position, glancing at him. He paused and looked at the other two men. One might survive if he had immediate medical attention. Silver didn't think that was an available option considering the distant shouts and screams from the complex.

He moved to the man with part of his face missing, stripped him of his belt with its knife and other gear, put it on, and picked up the weapon lying next to the dead man.

Silver moved to the door the men had come through. Looking through the small bars he saw the room beyond lay in shambles. The ceiling collapsed, and Silver realized the men probably would have been killed if they'd stayed in there.

He tried the doorknob and found it to be locked. One of the men probably had keys, but the way was impassable, anyway. They needed to find a different way out.

The ground shook again, and the building

rumbled and protested. Stones fell around Silver, and he hurried back to the cell.

A dust cloud filled the air; the outer wall had collapsed.

Hank stood staring at the sky outside.

Silver guided Hank to the makeshift rubble ramp and pushed her forward.

Once they were outside and in the evening air, Hank seemed to recover somewhat.

"We need to get out of here," Silver said.

"We need to get the Jazeer's Light," Hank said.

The two looked at one another.

Hank's face, set and determined, had small specks of red smeared across it where she'd wiped tears away. Silver searched her expression, and understood she needed to make sense of what happened, to give it a purpose and a reason for happening.

Silver nodded.

Travis I. Sivart

Chapter 21

They heard rotors spinning up, a helicopter preparing to leave, and moved towards it.

The compound was in chaos. The manicured gardens were a stark counterpoint to the crimson destruction in the sky, and the orange lava rivulets creeping down the side of Mount Etna.

Dozens of different makes and models of vehicles were screaming out of the complex, heading anywhere except for the hills. The hills only offered fiery death from the volcano. No one paid attention to two more people ducking and dodging as they tried to escape the disaster.

Hank grabbed Silver's arm and pointed at a white-suited figure heading for the helipad.

Silver nodded, and the two moved towards the figure, crouching.

Both Silver and Hank wrapped a wet cloth torn from clothing or curtains around their faces to help block out smoke and toxic fumes.

They moved closer, ducking behind a hedge sculpted into a maze, topiaries of animals standing in the center of clearings with benches around them. One elephant, rampant and on two legs with its trunk in the air, was on fire from a chunk of lava that had landed on it.

Aaron Roberts moved across the grass, a hundred meters from escaping the inferno. He was alone, his bodyguards fanning out to discourage others from approaching the whirlybird and trying to use it for their own getaway.

Hank raised her weapon and looked at it. She pulled the shoulder strap from over her head and threw it into the bushes. She crouched again and ran towards the man.

Silver watched her.

Hank's face was hard, and he guessed she was struggling to deal with what was in front of them, or collapse under the weight of what had happened behind them.

They closed the distance as Roberts straightened and began walking in a very calm, collected, and dignified manner towards his way out of this mess. The man in white carried a black satchel under one arm. Its rectangular shape suggested a hard case, and the way he clutched it suggested it was of immense value.

Roberts was the sort that always needed to look superior and in control. That was his schtick, the way he intimidated others. By seeming to know things they didn't, he triggered insecurities, thus making them feel awed and inspired by someone who was confident in dire circumstances.

Other people glanced at the man, shooting looks of panicked hatred at him. But they didn't approach him or interfere.

When Silver and Smith were within a dozen meters of Roberts, and twenty meters of the helicopter, Silver opened his mouth to get the man's attention.

"Hey, scumbag," Hank shouted, anger bubbled over in her words, "where the hell do you think you're going?"

Roberts turned, paling when he saw them.

Hank, blood-spattered, stalked towards him with

an almost maniacal purpose, fire in her eyes and danger in her movements. She held no weapons, but she had an air that spoke of a threat that needed nothing more than her glare.

Silver was a mess. He was in his black tactical pants and white tank top, an automatic weapon slung over his shoulder, and a belt of pouches around his waist. He was barefooted except for shredded socks. He limped from cuts on his feet from crossing broken masonry, stonework, and unsuccessfully dodging hot coals from various fires.

"You," Roberts sneered over his shoulder, slowing but not stopping, "haven't you enough sense to give up? You should just lay down and die, already."

Roberts bared his teeth and unconsciously pulled the satchel closer, like an animal protecting a hard-won morsel of food that meant its survival.

"You will fail," Hank growled, pointing at Roberts. "You will give us the lamp, and then you will run away like a scared rat to hide in some dark hole to lick your wounds. You won't come out until you can use your damned PR unit to spin this where you seem to be the victim and hero, even though you are neither."

Hank spat.

"But you are neither," she continued. "You're just a scavenger who uses unsubstantiated fear to get the better of those who did the real work."

"Shut up," Roberts said, his voice a whine that did nothing to belay Hank's accusations. "You're a broken little girl, trying to prove yourself, but never having the guts to do what really needs done to actually succeed."

Hank bent down, scooped a rock, and flung it unerringly at the man, without stopping her forward movement.

It struck Roberts in the temple.

The man flinched, his face screwing into a look of confusion, anger, and disbelief.

"What the hell do you think you're doing?" Roberts stopped and turned towards Hank, taking one step forward. "No one would dare strike me!"

"I dare," Hank yelled, her voice pitching high and frantic, "and I'm sick and tired of people like you who think they can do whatever they want, and the consequences be damned. You're being called out, and will pay for your actions, here and now, you stupid, scared little twit."

Roberts took a step backwards, towards the waiting helicopter.

Silver knew Hank had snapped. She wasn't wrong, and he agreed with everything she'd said, but this wasn't quite the approach he would have taken in this situation.

He was also glad he hadn't yet released his latest design for helicopters that allowed for instant and silent acceleration using magnetic propulsion.

Silver looked the man over, searching for weapons. Roberts was unarmed.

The helicopter, whose blades had now reached full speed, was ready for liftoff.

A new man stepped from the vehicle, dressed in all black. A black suit jacket with the sleeves rolled up, a black t-shirt underneath, dark hair slicked back, and his full beard oiled to a point. Jeweled rings decorated his fingers, and bracelets of jewels and precious metals hung from his wrists, and a single thick, gold-linked chain hung around his neck. The man stood tall, his shoulders back, and he gave off an air of competence.

It was Saman Kazemi.

Hank noticed him and hesitated.

Roberts saw their reactions to something behind him. He turned to see what they were looking at.

Saman strode forward in impossibly long strides, smiling, and reached for Roberts.

Taking the other man's head in his hands, Saman snapped Roberts's neck in one swift movement.

Grabbing Roberts's lapels in one fist, Saman held the white suited man up to keep him from falling, and lifted the satchel from his limp form with his other hand. Then he released Roberts, who collapsed to the ground, dead.

"Hello, my friends," Saman looked a little embarrassed speaking to Hank and Silver, "you have done well. I now have the artifact of my people and will return it to its proper place. Glory be to my people, who shall rally with its return and rise to their proper place in things."

Hank let out a long, keening whine, watching Roberts fall at the feet of Saman.

Silver's gun jerked up to his shoulder and his head tilted as he lined up the sight.

"You can't," Silver shouted.

"I can, and I will," Saman's voice came from everywhere, as if he were standing beside them, and using a speaker system.

"I called upon the volcano, dear, sweet, Etna," the disembodied voice said, "to assist me. I demanded the elements to heed my call, to respond to my demands, to overcome the petty technology and egos of this modern world, and return to me what was properly mine."

A trail of smoke and ash wafted between the two

and the helicopter, concealing Saman.

"I wish you both health and prosperity, my friends," Saman said, and Hank and Silver felt the light touch of a finger on their foreheads. "I offer you the fortune of fate and blessing of luck in all you do."

Silver hesitated, wanting to make sure he had a clear shot.

"It is done," Saman's voice was a distant whisper on the wind. "I bring the Jazeer's Light to the land of its birth, and return it to the place it belongs."

The fingers of volcanic distraction moved away, like a god playing peek-a-boo and moving its hands away from its hidden face.

The helicopter was high above them, and a feminine figure stood where it had been.

Joan looked at the crumbled form of Roberts, then brought up her rifle as she saw them.

"I didn't think you had it in you," Joan sneered, looking at Hank who now stood over Roberts's prone form.

"I didn't?" Hank's reply was confused, unsure.

"That'd be easier to believe," Joan said, "but I don't see anyone else close enough to give credit, so it must have been you."

Joan's weapon jerked and the crack of gunfire followed. She had Hank directly in her sights, and there was no way the shot would miss from a dozen meters away.

The last trailers of smoke dissipated, and Hank stood there, staring down at herself, looking for the inevitable wounds.

But there weren't any.

Silver squeezed his trigger, aiming at the same spot he'd targeted when Saman stood there.

Joan's right shoulder jerked backwards, and her rifle went flying into the smoke.

Silver fired again and again. Short, controlled shots, conserving ammunition and making sure each shot was true and not altered by recoil.

The woman tumbled backwards off the hill where she'd stood, rolling out of sight.

Hank darted forward, but Silver's hand on her shoulder restrained her.

"Leave me alone," Hank shouted, trying to pull from his gentle grip.

"Do you want to see?" Silver asked. "Or have you seen enough tonight? Maybe she's dead, and you can see her dead, staring corpse. Or maybe she's alive, and can make her way to someone who'll help her."

Hank turned to look at Silver, her eyes wet and full.

"What do you do if you get to her and she's alive?" Silver asked. "Do you help her? Kill her? Leave her to her fate?"

Hank quivered as the words hit her.

"Maybe we should find our own way out?" Silver said. "We still have the Jazeer's Light to track down and return to a museum. Maybe that's what we should focus on right now? Getting out of here and completing the job we were hired to do?"

Hank's body wracked, shaking with too much emotion, but no tears fell.

She nodded, and Silver turned her to the east, and towards the direction the helicopter had flown.

"Here's where we're going," Hank said dully,

poking at her cardphone.

The two had made their way out of the complex and to the Catania Fontanarossa Airport where Silver's jet waited.

It had been impounded, and the tired clerk at the counter told them that the people who owned it were wanted for questioning by INTERPOL in matters regarding a theft of some stupid antique.

The woman hadn't even looked up from her magazine until they thanked her and turned to leave. She thought nothing about the two except it was nice that a daughter helped her father who had problems walking.

The two caught a commercial flight going to Tehran, Iran, using identities that Silver cobbled together from his private resources.

Hank poked at her cardphone and a map appeared, a red dot forming over Catania, then another over Tehran, and a red line crept across the screen spanning the Mediterranean Sea, stopping at Adana, Turkey for a layover, then continuing on to Tehran, Iran. From there, it showed a dotted line of a smaller airline flying them almost directly south, but slightly east, to Shiraz.

Chapter 22

They landed in Shiraz, got a hotel, outfitted themselves, rested overnight, and rented a car the following day. On the flight over, Hank did some research using what Saman said as a starting point.

Return the Jazeer's Light to the land of its birth: that was Persia. The closest place Hank figured Saman would take the artifact was Persepolis, once the richest cities in the world and the seat of power of the Achaemenid Empire. A second option would be Naqsh-e Rustam, the necropolis and resting place of four of the most powerful men in ancient history.

"What about Cyrus?" Silver asked.

"King Cyrus's resting place is nearby," Hank explained, "and as a side note, it's also one of the earliest earthquake-proof structures known. It's a small standalone structure, but Saman is more likely to head for one of the other two points on the map."

"Why?" Silver asked as they drove along the Shiraz-Marvdasht Highway, moving northeast towards their destinations. "Why does he want to bring some scrap-metal oil lamp to a dead city in the middle of the desert?"

"It's either symbolic," Hank's tone was the same as a university professor, who's passionate about what they teach, "because one is where all the power was and the other is where all the power died and continues to rest, or he actually believes in the magic of the lamp."

"What?" Silver glanced at her out of the corner of his eye. "Like, you think, Saman actually believes in genies and that rubbing the lamp can grant three wishes and all that?"

"I don't know if 'believe' is the right word," Hank said slowly, turning to look out the window.

She fell quiet, and Silver waited for her to continue.

The inside of the car was AC cooled, but warmth radiated through, and magnified by, the windshield and windows. The black dashboard collected and exuded heat. The temperature outside was intense and would reach thirty Celsius even though it was a cool October and had dropped to fifteen Celsius the previous night.

Beige landscape with the distant, faded orange of rock outcroppings dominated the view, dotted with green scrub bushes. The vegetation was thick near the road where it had irrigation, but it was a desolate land a kilometer from the asphalt, where sand hawks and lizards hunted and basked in the sun.

"Did you know," Hank said suddenly, "that tomorrow, the twenty-ninth, is Cyrus the Great Day?"

Silver shook his head.

Noticing the movement in the window reflection Hank turned to look at him, waiting for an answer.

"So?" Silver shrugged.

"That means tomorrow is an almost holy day," Hank explained, speaking as she would to a child, or a slow student, "like the Yanks' Fourth of July, or the birthday of their first president. You aren't from the states, are you, Silver?"

Silver shrugged again.

"I'm from near them," he said in a neutral tone.

"In regard to djinni," Hank said, switching topical

gears again, "did you know they predate the Bible? They're in the Jewish mythos, the Christian mythos, and the Muslim mythos. They aren't angels, or demons, but something else. They live, eat, defecate, and breed like people, but can live for thousands of years. And God told them they must obey and bow to Adam and his descendants. They have to follow the commands of humans."

Silver stared ahead, waiting for Hank to go on.

"But they're tricky buggers," Hank said after a few minutes of silence, "and often fool us mere mortals into doing what they want. Did you notice how he's changed each time?"

Silver waited, and then realized Hank was watching and waiting for him to answer her question.

"Who?" Silver asked, turning to look at her twice in quick succession.

"Saman, you simpleton," Hank said with a laugh that faded into a sigh that felt mildly disdainful, "every time we saw him, he looked a little different. He changed, and not just his clothes, but his attitude, and more. I swear he's gotten taller and better built. And all this in just a couple of weeks? It ain't natural. So, how do you explain it?"

"Clothes make the man?" Silver offered, pulling his sun visor down and spinning it to block the sun out the side window. "I know lots of people that seem different depending on what clothes they're wearing. It's like switching costumes and becoming a different character to some people. Maybe that's all he's doing?"

"Perhaps," Hank said slowly, "but perhaps not. How does he constantly appear where we are, know what our next move is, and how he's also done that to others, like Roberts?"

Silver moved off the Shiraz-Marvdasht highway and merged into traffic on the Marvdasht-Sa'adatshahr Expressway.

"How?" Silver's question felt like a lead into an explanation. "It's a world of surveillance now. Companies track every person to know what to advertise to them, and it wouldn't be too hard for someone with money and resources to track us. Knowing where people are, and what they want, is a currency in itself in this day and age."

"Yeah," Hank nodded, "that's probably it. And this man, Saman Kazemi, has tracked and predicted our every move without a visible crime family around him. He's done what the trillionaire Roberts couldn't do, without the resources Roberts had."

"Are you suggesting that Saman is using magic?"

"You said it yourself, Silver," Hank looked the man in the eye, her expression dead serious, "you've seen things that normal means can't explain. There's more in this world than can be explained, whether or not it was there through all of history. Perhaps it disappeared for a few centuries or millennia and is coming back."

They drove along in silence for a long time after that.

Their first stop was the Ruins of Persepolis, which had been the dazzling capital of the Achaemenid Empire. They parked at the corner of Persepolis Street in the parking lot of a small convenience store across from Pardis Park and the ruins. They set out at a good pace, both wearing a shawl to cover them from the biting wind, the harsh sun, and prying eyes.

"These avenues we're walking along were in their glory two and a half millennium ago," Hank said, slowing. "They were uncovered and restored through decades of hard work on the part of archeologists, interns, and students. They're the same paths peasants and emperors walked, in awe and in mundane tasks."

She sighed, smiling.

"We're passing through the Gate of Nations," she explained, pointing out the sights. "The Apadana Palace is there, on the right, with the Hadish Palace behind it, and we'll be entering the Throne room, and then into the Treasury."

Each area was enormous, any of them larger than a football field, of the American sort or the proper sort. Cropped columns and perfectly straight walls dotted the area.

"They reconstructed some parts as it was in the days of glory," Hank continued the impromptu tour, "giving us snapshot dioramas of what had once stood there. It's amazing."

Hundreds of people milled about, moving slowly, in groups or individually. They stared up at the ancient structures in awe and a few raised cameras or phones to snap photos. The rising wind pulled away any conversations that were more than a few meters from the two.

"This was once the richest and most opulent cities on the planet," Hank sighed; it sounded more like overwhelmed wonder than anything else. "We're within a couple minutes' walk of the Tombs of Artaxerxes the second and the third, descendants of the infamous Xerxes that we hear so much about. And though it is thought that the first Xerxes may have lost his life and throne to his son through less than honorable means, they were still rulers of an empire that was magnificent."

Hank looked around. To the casual observer, it looked like she was taking in her surroundings, not much different than one of the hundreds of other people here. But Silver saw the squint, the focus, the passion and the drive in her eyes. Her head moved smoothly, stopping suddenly, and her eyes darting around an area. She was looking for something specific.

"What, exactly, are we looking for here?" Silver asked, shoving his hands in his pockets, looking past her at a line of chipped and broken stone, ten-meter-high marble columns, and various statues of mythological beasts, long dead heroes, and kings.

"The things that don't belong here," Hank said, her voice stopping and starting as she spun in a slow circle, "things that are old, but too new, or too well put together for something that's thousands of years old. Saman must have done something here, left some clue, even if this isn't where the end ceremony will be."

"Ceremony?" Silver asked, watching an Iranian duo of police turn towards them.

Dozens of clumps of people stood between them and the officers, but the two men were looking directly at Hank, not even seeming to notice Silver looming at her side.

"Yes, a ceremony," Hank muttered, looking up at the tops of the pillars, scanning the uppermost parts of the ancient statues, "these sorts of things, these beings—I would assume, not that I've met many, or any at all really, considering they haven't existed recently enough to even be considered more than legend—they love a ceremony. Words, motions, ritual, all these things carry power and meaning. It's those things that connect the meaning and intention to the power."

Silver tore his eyes away from the approaching Iranian Gendarmerie and looked at Hank. She was in her zone. Her eyes were distant, but not like she wasn't totally there, more like she was more there than ever, and totally focused on what she was seeking.

"And I think," she continued, "that Saman Kazemi, djinni or ifrit, would have stopped here and tied this place of power into his network. Bringing in the energy of faith, belief, wonder, and logic that has been overlaid in these ruins would be of great help to him."

"The energy of logic?" Silver said, searching the crowd again for the police. "Does that make any sense at all?"

"Logic is a form of faith," Hank explained, drawing out her cardphone and pulling up an app, "it's belief based on what you've been told or learned. It just happens, usually but not always, to be based on facts and proofs. But it's still a faith because you believe it to be true for your own reasons, or perhaps because of your reason itself. Religion isn't so different. People believe it to be true because they were told its true by someone they trust. To the faithful, religion is logic. And I'm testing for electric and magnetic fluxes, trying to pinpoint what he did."

"Um, Hank," Silver put his hand on her shoulder, trying to get her attention, "I think you should wrap this up now. I believe we've gotten some attention by those who are faithful."

"What're you talking about, Silver?" Hank didn't

look up from her cardphone. "I've attached a specialized sensor to help me find the subtle radiation of the energy I'm looking for. I've almost got it. Give me just another couple seconds."

"I don't know if we have that long, Hank." Silver let go of her shoulder.

Iran didn't allow firearms into the country, so Silver and Hank had to make do in other ways.

Silver pulled out two long blades, too short to be swords, but too long to be knives. Each blade was longer than his forearm, and gleamed with an unnaturally sharp edge, machine sharpened and laser honed.

Hank looked at him, confusion crossing her face for the barest moment, before understanding dawned.

She smiled.

"Oh," she breathed, "those poor bastards, they shall rue getting between me and the revealing of an ancient power source."

Hank unbuttoned her sleeves, rolling them up her arms, and rebuttoning them above the elbow using a cloth strap under the sleeve, in an old-fashioned style.

The lawmen made their way through the crowd towards the two. The people the police passed paused in their conversations, turned in the direction that the two officers were moving, and fixed their now silent stares on Hank. The mass of tourists began falling in behind the two men, like sand in an hourglass, following the first two grains through the neck, and flowing behind them.

"Ohhh feck," Hank growled, "it's a trap, Silver. Saman lured us here, meaning to stop any pursuit that might try to follow him."

"Ya think?" The sarcasm in Silver's voice was as

thick as cold oatmeal. "I don't think the people coming towards us know why they're doing what they're doing. I don't want to hurt them, Hank. I hope they're just a delaying technique. Well, the bottom line is that I don't want to trigger yet another international event between Iran and the west by attacking their authorities. I'll try to subdue them and not kill them. Anyway, that's always a good idea whenever available. Did you get anything from the reading?"

The athletic man fell into a defensive stance, his weapons held in front of him.

"Oh, let me check before we have to deal with magical mind zombies, and they do look like that, don't they?" Hank looked down at her cardphone, checking readings, as she continued to hypothesize about the approaching horde of people lumbering towards them, "I think that the mass of humanity that's coming at us might have a wee effect on my triangulation calculations to help find Saman. Do you think you could just knock them all unconscious, and that might let me get a cleaner reading?"

"Really, Hank?" Silver exclaimed. "You want me to knock dozens of people—hell, it might be a hundred or more—unconscious, so you can check your phone?"

"Yah," Hank smiled, "you're catching on now, Silver. Take care of that, would you?"

She laughed, and rolled her eyes, the whites showing as her humor turned a bit maniacal and hysterical.

The younger woman slapped at her various pockets and pouches, looking for anything that might help. She saw Silver had twin blades drawn and thought for a moment to discourage him from seriously injuring anyone. On second thought, which followed immediately on the heels of her first thought, Silver was a big boy and could take care of himself and make his own decisions.

Pulling cuffs from a larger pouch at her hip—each about three fingers wide and less than one thick—Hank slapped the devices around her wrists. They clicked into place, and the cyber-installs within them synced to her pulse and muscle movements. The instruments, designed by her for defensive measures when on dangerous digs, were made to fire small chemical darts meant to stun aggressive predators.

Her hands came up, and she sighted down her forearms.

The crowd rushing forward threatened to overwhelm them.

Silver despised those that attacked or hurt anyone who couldn't defend themselves. These people, in his mind, were unable to stand up to him or his level of ability.

The attackers were pale, a look of terror and confusion on their face that betrayed that they didn't understand why they were attacking two people.

Silver's swords shot out, the flat clapping against ears and the sides of heads, causing them to collapse to the ground, stunned. He moved like a dervish, swirling through the crowd. Thin slices appeared on foreheads, hands, and fatty parts of bodies such as hips, outer thighs, and buttocks.

The people, not inclined to violence, either fainted on the spot, or turned away after receiving an injury. The ones with aggressive natures hesitated when their blood flowed. Many of both types turned and fled.

Hank thrust her wrists forward and her capsulized

air propulsion system shot small darts into necks, inner thighs, and the crook of people's elbows. Hank aimed for easily accessible blood vessels to introduce the anesthetizing chemical to the attackers' bloodstreams.

Within thirty seconds, dozens of people lay in a semi-circle around Hank and Silver, or were stumbling away, gripping various cuts and lacerations.

The two officers stood in front of the two, legs spaced equal to their shoulders in a firing stance, eyes sighting down their dominant arms, and guns held steady in front of them.

"Okay!" Silver shouted, and their eyes darted to him, "you got us. I'm about to drop my weapons on the ground for you to see!"

The men shifted slightly, turning to cover the mercenary.

Silver held both swords directly in front of him, tips pointing skyward, and then twisting his grip. The blades fell point down. He caught them so he was holding them with his fingertips and pointing towards the ground.

One of Hank's darts bit into the necks of each guard. The men's heads whipped towards the woman, causing their equilibrium to throw them off balance. The men swayed and tumbled sideways, their eyes rolling back.

Silver flipped his weapons again, and they popped back into place as he turned his wrists and tightened his grip.

The remaining people slowed, then stopped, as if waking up from a sleepwalking episode. They backed away, looking at the dozens of people on the ground. Some turned and ran, pulling out phones to film video—or to call authorities, but probably the former—and others just turned away and walked in the other direction casually, as if they didn't want to attract the attention of whoever did this.

Hank's cardphone beeped. She lifted her wrist and looked at it.

"I've got it," Hank said, looking west. "I think the people breaking free did it, but it triangulated him to the west. Right over Naqsh-e Rustam."

Chapter 23

The wind grew stronger, tearing at plants in the sandy soil and whipping sand drifts up to dance along the dunes. Dust devils, no taller than a man, skirted the road and followed the car for a short distance, then dropped from existence just as quickly. The sun played peek-a-boo behind wafting clouds, disappearing and reappearing in the thickening weather as the temperature dropped.

Sand scoured the side of the car and gusts buffeted the vehicle, causing it to jerk to one side. A tumbleweed—known as Anastatica, commonly called as the flower of Mariyam or Russian thistle weed, Hank explained—darted between traffic, bouncing off an antique model 2022 sports car, and disappearing into the scrub growth on the other side. As they drove, the frequency and size of the plant's appearance increased, as if nature itself were running towards something, or away.

The sky darkened in the northwest, the direction they headed, and lightning tumbled and played in the thick, rounded clouds above the horizon. Traffic was heavy and slow, as if everyone decided they needed to be out today but didn't quite know where they were going. Cars glutted the highway, as if they wanted to go to important historical landmarks.

After passing Naqsh-e Rajab—a small roadside area that comprised a handful of relief carvings, named for the man who protected them while running a coffee shop about a century ago—they turned left onto Marv Dasht-Sarooie Road towards Naqsh-e Rustam.

Two men with a herd of a hundred or more goats, all dun and rust colored, stood on the side of the highway. They turned to watch them pass from behind dark sunglasses.

Traffic thinned the closer they got to Naqsh-e Rustam, and the haboob—that's the type of sandstorm they were driving through, Hank explained to Silver—intensified and grew to cover the entire horizon from east to west. Soon, they were travelling at a crawl to make sure they stayed on the disappearing road as it covered with sand.

The lightning was more frequent now, blinding Silver, who was still driving, causing him to see photo-negative images of the surrounding storm and terrain. All around them, the sky filled with sand and dust that swirled and buffeted them inside the car, as if it were attacking them with soft, rounded claws made of wind and angry intent.

It started to rain. At first Silver and Hank thought it was sleet. A light tinkling sound bouncing off the car's hood and roof, small crystalline beads collecting along the windshield wipers.

"Wow," Silver leaned forward and looked upward through the windshield as they crept towards their destination, "the lightning, it's turning the sand particulates into glass."

"That's impossible," Hank's head whipped towards the passenger window, "nothing like that has ever been reported."

"I guess no one has ever seen a djinni in action," Silver muttered.

Hank's window hummed as she lowered it enough

to stick her hand out of it, leaning backwards, tiny shards flying inside the car.

She drew her hand back inside and rolled the window up. Small glass beads, the size of silica pearls in the stay-dry packs you get inside of a bottle of pills, lined her palm in addition to dozens of small cuts inflicted by the odd weather.

"This is mythical level stuff," Hank's voice was awed. "Raiders of the Lost Ark or Biblical plague sort of stuff."

Lightning flashed, causing ten thousand scintillating prism rainbows to dance in the air for a fraction of a second before dissipating into the photo-negative sight it left behind.

Naqsh-e Rustam rose in front of the car, and they parked in the tourist parking lot with less than a handful of cars in it. The monument was barely visible in the distance, a half kilometer away.

Hank reached behind the driver's seat and into the back seat of the car. Bringing forward a bulging satchel, she handed Silver a pair of wide, padded goggles that allowed peripheral vision, a breathing mask that covered nose and mouth, and his scarf to wrap around and cover everything those two things didn't. They checked their gear one last time, then swung the doors open and left the car.

The weather slackened a bit when Hank and Silver entered the protected area where the wind cut off in the monument's lee. Dark clouds roiled above, moving as if alive or inhabited by giant celestial serpents of smoke and dust.

Hank thought back to Mount Etna, the volcano near Catania, and noticed similarities in the movement of the two cloud formations.

Naqsh-e Rustam was an incredible display of artistry and craftsmanship from an era centuries before the Julian calendar and more than a millennium before Christians even conceived the Gregorian calendar. It was the tomb of four of the greatest rulers of the Persian Empire. Darius I had been confirmed and archeologists believed that Xerxes I, Artaxerxes I, and Darius II were also entombed here before the tombs were raided and razed. A fifth tomb had been started, and plans for two others had been discovered, but had never come to fruition.

Persian crosses a dozen meters tall and wide had been carved meters-deep into the rock face, and relief carvings of conquering kings, mighty heroes, famous generals, and fallen foes bracketed the columned entrances of the yellowed beige stone of each tomb.

Three people stood in front of each tomb, spaced evenly along the cross section of the open carved face; one in the center, and one to each side of the first, and facing outward, away from the tombs. Their hands were raised high above their heads and their legs spread to shoulder width, creating an hourglass shape with their bodies.

"It's a ritual," Hank shouted, leaning closer to Silver so he could hear her over the wind, "a Zoroastrian ritual similar to the ceremony they did over the deceased before placing them in a Tower of Silence. But it's wrong, it's backwards. It's like they're reversing the ritual."

Wind gusted outward from the tombs, whistling and wailing out of the cave-like sepulcher mouths, braiding together to form a solid wind-rope that shot outward. It came straight towards Silver and Hank, the two diving to opposite sides, before it veered to the left towards a small rectangular building about fifty meters from the mountain of mausoleums.

The two turned towards the building.

"The Ka'ba-ye Zartosht," said Hank, moving up to Silver. His look of confusion made her go on. "It translates to 'the Cube of Zoroaster.'"

The Cube of Zoroaster sat in a cleared out square, the part visible from where Hank stood looked like the cube of its name. The building was the same time-washed, beige-yellow of all the surrounding structures that had been sun-bleached and weathered for almost two and a half millennia. Smaller rectangular indents and windows dotted the four walls.

The indent the edifice squatted in hid another third of its height, and wide, thick stairs led from the bottom of the pit to the only door in the structure.

Four people, one at each corner, stood over the pit, their hands held high also. A single man stood atop the structure. He wore a black suit with slacks and a double-breasted jacket, his muscular chest and broad shoulders well defined as the wind pressed against him. When the wind shifted, so did his outfit, and often looked like the traditional thobe of the people of this region with long-flowing sleeves. He had a full beard, silver accenting his temples and streaking his facial hair. His hair was pulled back and to the top of his head in a bun.

"Saman Kazemi," Silver muttered, and then said it louder so Hank could hear him over the rushing air, "he's changed again, and not just his outfit."

Thick grey mist swirled around Saman, coiling about him like an air serpent one moment, and the next moment making his suit jacket look like a billowing bisht, or cloak, whipping it around his powerful form.

"You think?" Hank's sarcasm was easily heard over the wind.

Saman looked down at the two, his eyes lighting with the purple-white crackle and glow of the lightning.

Chapter 24

Saman looked like he was almost three meters tall atop the twelve-meter Cube of Zoroaster. He was an impressive figure, with eyes of lightning and a cloak of cloud, his face contorted in concentration and emotion, his body wracked with waves of the sensation of magical evolution, changing more in a handful of minutes than most people would in a decade of life.

The people around the square pit didn't move from the four corners, standing still and enraptured, with their arms held high. The wind didn't touch these people, but thin streaks of lightning shot down at them, into them, and then burst forward in a sudden torrent to wash over Saman like an angry wave on a hurricane-swathed shore.

Saman's hands were thrust upward, the small and antiquated oil lamp hovering above him, between his outspread arms. It glowed, sparks spearing outward and shattering on the surrounding mist of clouds, raining purple-white energy down on him.

The creature, for he was no longer a mere man, on top of the ancient structure of secrets, turned to look at Silver. He paused, sizing him up and taking in everything that was the man.

Silver felt exposed, stripped of all secrets and self. It was as if this thing that was once an apologetic and meek boy was now some sort of god-like being able to disassemble Silver in a look, taking him down to his component parts, and knowing each fear, hope, dream, and insecurity that made up the mind and psyche, the very soul, that was Silver.

Silver let out a stream of breath as the man moved his gaze to Hank.

Hank flinched but didn't do much else.

Silver watched Saman do the same to the woman and had to wonder…was Hank stronger than he was? Was she made of sterner stuff than Silver?

Hank stiffened when Saman's gaze locked onto her. The djinni's vision dug into her, seeking her core and her essence. She fought, but not by putting up a wall or pushing back. She moved, not in a physical way, but with her mind, with her heart, with everything that was her. Hank writhed and contorted without ever moving a muscle, sliding out of the direct perception this creature of ages past that had been created before mankind was even a thought.

Hank laughed.

It was a small laugh. More of a snicker, than anything else. She didn't guffaw in a mocking way; she didn't let out a derisive snort of laughter. She giggled, like she had a secret and no one else could know it without her telling them.

Saman's face contorted.

"Why," his voice was deep and reverberated off the canyon walls, but still had that undertone of humbleness that Saman had when they first met back in the coffee shop in London, "do you deny me what I seek?"

"Oh," Hank's voice still carried an amused tone, "I'll be happy to tell you that, but only after you answer a few questions for me. Do we have an accord?"

Saman rocked back, now floating a meter off the ground, as if she'd struck him. Surprise flowed across his face.

"An accord," his answer was a spoken fact, and the word rolled as if he were tasting it to see if he liked it.

"Yes," Hank smiled, covering the grimace of pain in her head, struggling to not release her thoughts, hopes, and fears to this being, "you know, those things you've been doing with folks for a couple thousand years? You should know about making a deal, or have you forgotten since you've been human?"

"No," Saman's voice was slow in response, and rumbled like distant thunder when he did reply, "I understand, and I agree. I will allow you questions three."

"Really?" Hank tilted her head and made a face that looked like she just sipped vinegar.

"With this you disagree?" the djinni asked.

"No," Hank shrugged, "I'm just wondering why you said it in rhyme. Isn't that a bit, well, fairy-tale like? I mean, you're speaking in English, and it's not even your native language, and you decide to do in rhyme? I call shenanigans."

"I speak to the listeners," Saman's answer was smooth and confident. "My words are created so the one hearing them can understand and relate to them best. That is one question, technically two questions, but we will call it one, since I am kind and generous. What are your other two?"

"Oh, damn it!" Hank slapped her forehead and winced from the jarring of her brain, "I fell right into that one."

Hank cut off her words before they became another question.

"Okay then," she cocked her head, "second

question, why did you choose the Ka'ba-ye Zartosht?"

The air went out of Saman as if someone had punched him in the solar plexus. His head snapped towards her, his eyes blazing in their focus on her. He ignored the man beside Hank now, who was side-stepping and creeping away from the human woman.

Usually, throughout history, humans had been easy to manipulate, even when he wasn't connected to the source of his power. They wanted to be led; they wanted to be handed something to believe. They prayed for it.

And even the ones that rose up, and fought against such things, really only wanted the same thing, but with the added reassurance that they weren't sheep and what they were following was new, original, and not normal. It was so easy to direct and manipulate mankind into doing whatever Saman needed done.

He saw no reason to not share the information with the woman, knowing this information would make her feel special and different, as if she had achieved something no one else could. He would allow her that.

"This place, this Cube of Zoroaster, has been said to hold many things. Some say it held the everlasting holy fire, lit to represent eternity and all the passion and wisdom that can be experienced. Others have conjectured that it held volumes of knowledge that were far too expansive to fit within the confines of its walls. Others have thought it was a solar calendar and observatory. And still others have thought it was a simple grave site."

Saman paused and waited.

Hank watched him, her lips twitching, itching with the questions she wanted to ask, but she wouldn't take the bait the djinni had laid out.

When she didn't ask another question, he went on, a tinge of frustration in his voice.

"The Ka'ba-ye Zartosht was where I placed an item of power," Saman glared at her, spitting the words out, one by one, "infused with my being and essence, and because of that, much of my magic."

"Oh," Hank ran her fingers through her hair, "so it was a prison of sorts, and they had the important bits of you trapped there. I bet they tricked you to put them there. That's how it normally works."

"No," Saman said, "I chose to put it there because of an agreement. They freed certain people, letting them go their way without further harassment, because I agreed to this. That was your third question, and our game is done. Now you shall pay your price."

"Oh, no you don't," Hank waggled a finger at the creature, "I didn't ask any questions. I made a series of conjectured statements, and you offered the information following of your own free will."

Hank smiled when the djinni turned his head back to look at her.

"You're really out of practice, and I bet this is because you were so long separated from that bit of you, that essence of your very being, that makes you what you are," Hank chose her words carefully, making sure she used statements rather than questions. She'd gained this skill when writing thesis papers. Professors always counted it against you when you asked more questions, but they liked it when you turned those questions into statements of fact about the things that aren't yet known.

Silver sidled towards the stationary people standing on the edge of the pit. Approaching, he noticed that the odd glass shards created by the lightning in the haboob wasn't affecting them and cutting them to ribbons as it did to Hank's hand.

Saman didn't answer Hank. His body twitched with spasms, and the energy from the lightning now seemed to be issuing from the Cube of Zoroaster and coursing into him.

The lamp slowly descended from above him until it was between his feet, but still hovering above the stone of the building.

"Ask your third question." Saman stared straight ahead, speaking with breathless pants.

"Oh," Hank sighed—letting out a breath she never even realized she was holding—and smiled, but it was wane and distracted as she watched Saman's reactions. "I'm working on it, and shall ask very soon. But time for a being such as yourself shouldn't matter very much. I could take weeks, months, or even years, and it shouldn't matter to you."

Silver moved to the people on the corners of the pit and disabled them, wrapping an arm around their windpipe from behind and cutting off their oxygen supply until they slumped unconscious to the desert floor. He recognized the second and third people he disabled as the two he'd first met in his warehouse in London.

Hank thought, trying to decide what question she could ask that would end this. Or at least, what question would change the outcome from a legendary being regaining a power beyond human comprehension to something more manageable.

"Well?" Saman thrust the question forward, pushing her to answer and making it clear that he wouldn't wait forever for the next query.

"Oh, shut it," Hank snapped, glaring at the man glowing and hovering above the ancient structure. "You didn't say I had to ask them within a certain amount of time."

"I also didn't say," Saman countered, "that I wouldn't do anything—for example, rain fire and destruction across the land or even the entire world—while waiting for your lame questions."

"Fair point," Hank said swiftly. "Thank you for your patience. I shall endeavor to come up with my last question quickly. But you have waited two-thousand and five-hundred years, give or take, so I am guessing a few extra minutes while I collect my thoughts wouldn't be too much to ask."

Hank smiled at Saman.

The djinni laughed. It was a genuine laugh, and one that spoke of kinship and understanding.

"To quote you," Saman said, his face dropping into a serious look, "fair point. But on the other hand, I have waited millennia and centuries for this moment. Why would I wait a moment longer for the sake of someone who I have only known for mere moments of my existence?"

"Fine then," Hank huffed, "why would you sacrifice yourself for someone else, and what would it take for you to not change the world drastically or too suddenly?"

"That is two questions," Saman smiled. "I shall answer the first..."

"No," Hank's voice was crisp and cut through his words, "you said to 'ask my questions', so I did. I didn't take advantage of you by asking a dozen questions in one breath, instead I asked two. I feel that's fair since you cheated me of the first one anyway. And I asked one question that is all about you, and a second question that suggests cooperation and compromise."

"This is fair," Saman nodded after a moment's pause, his lips quirking into a brief smile as he stared sightlessly at the tombs in front of him. "I will answer both questions."

"One moment," Hank interrupted him, "I wasn't finished. Didn't your mother teach you any manners? Did you even have a mother? Never mind, strike those questions. I was still talking, and since I might be dead in a few seconds from now, I think you should listen to what I have to say."

Chapter 25

Saman bobbed, trying to turn and look at Hank, but the surrounding power held him in almost perfect stillness as it filled him from above and below.

"I don't want to see you destroyed," Hank began, hesitating as she spoke. "I've lived my whole life wanting to see one such as yourself. Not to be in awe—though I honestly am quite impressed by what I'm seeing—or to have something to worship. I've wanted something akin to this moment, just to know that there's more to the world, to life, to the universe, than the dull monotone, black and white, of science and history. I want hope, and amazement, and even a little fear and nervousness about what else is out there. I want there to be more than just what we know."

Hank took a deep breath, and realized the winds, sand, and storm had slowed around her. She pulled the breathing mask off her nose and mouth, but left the scarf up.

"But before we truly enter this duel of wits," she continued, "I want to know if I'm battling for the existence of mankind and our freedom, or if I'm battling against the freedom of a unique creature that adds another layer and dimension to reality as I know it. I need to know these things, Saman. I really, really hope you can understand that."

The wind howled in the silence, one moment a gentle careening noise, the next a sharp whistle cutting the corner of rock and stone.

"Your first question, why would I sacrifice myself for someone else, is a tale in itself that was three millennia in the making. Other beings of my people, like Iblis, who later went by the name Shaitan, roamed the lands. They had a vendetta and wanted to prove that we were superior to man. And I agree with them, on one level. We had more abilities, and that made us superior. But men, who were so much weaker and less gifted, overcame more challenges than we ever even imagined existed. That was a gift. To overcome in a place that others couldn't even see the challenge of life, that made man a special animal."

Saman paused, turning his head to look at the fallen followers at his feet, then to the twelve men and women in front of the tombs who still stood in the human cross formations to channel the powers long held back from him, into his form.

He shook his head, then waved his hand. Each person of the ritual fell limp like a puppet with its strings cut, including the unconscious ones at the corners of the pit of Ka'ba-ye Zartosht.

Silver stumbled backwards as the people he had incapacitated woke.

The newly awakened people rubbed at their eyes and coughed in the swirling dust.

"Help them, Silver," Saman said, his voice sounding almost as normal as it had when they'd first met, but tired, "get them scarves, and help them to their cars. I will shelter you from the storm as you do this task for me. I promise you this."

Silver stared upward at the being that Hank had distracted, and realized that the girl—no, the woman— had done much more than distract a being of power beyond science and understanding. She had engaged him. Silver's face slowly grew into a smile as he looked at Hank.

Hank looked at Silver, her face surprised when his face changed as she looked at him. He had a look of respect and amusement. It was a look you gave to an equal, not some kid tagging along on your adventure.

Silver nodded at Hank, still smiling.

Hank raised her hand a little, hesitantly, and waved at Silver.

"I helped man trap my people here," Saman said, "Dozens of ifrit, djinn, and other creatures, elemental in nature, and neither what your religious texts and scholars would call angels or demons, had been imprisoned in this place so man could have a chance to move forward. Things you called demons, like Ornias and Beelzebul, and other creatures who could teleport, control the minds of men, create illusions so real that men believed them to the last detail, shapeshift into any form real or imagined, become invisible and move about so no man would even suspect…they were in the room. All locked away. All trapped. All so your species and people could have a chance to show the creator what you could do.

"But now," Saman continued, "thousands of years later, I see that man has squandered his opportunities. He has had glorious advances, created wonders that would make my people gasp in awe. But he has also warred and fought with his own people, killing in the name of hate because someone was just a little different or because they believed the same thing but used a different manner to define it.

"I have watched man," Saman sounded sad, "as he moved from the barest of civilization to glorious cities that rise into the sky, as he destroyed the very soil and rivers that sustained him. He has shat into the hands and hearts of the very world and people that raised their voices in his glory, desecrating the faith that he has put into himself.

"It is time now," Saman's head jerked upwards, and the surrounding energies tripled in strength, "it is time now, to bring back that which was locked away.

"To answer your first question, I would sacrifice myself to give those with promise a chance to flourish. To answer your second question," Saman paused, and stepped forward and off the building.

The being that Saman had become stepped onto the air in front of him. The lightnings swirled, becoming a purple-white whirlwind of energy around him, crystalizing the dust and sand into a glass cone that fell under the inevitable power of gravity to crash and shatter on the ground below him, again and again.

Hank jumped when Silver touched her elbow. She turned and looked at him, eyebrows raised.

Her face spoke of concern, or worry, or wonder. She didn't have to speak, because it mirrored Silver's own feelings.

"Do we destroy him?" Silver asked, his voice clear in the air between repeated crashing of glass cones to the ground under Saman. "Or do we let him bring back what was an extinct species and allow it to rise again?"

"You know what's he offering, don't you?" Hank asked.

"Um," Silver hesitated, "is that rhetorical? He's offering to bring back a very angry race of super beings. And though I can't disagree with his logic, it feels a bit suicidal for our whole species for us to not try to stop him."

"Magic!" Hank yelled, raising her head over Silver's shoulder and directing the word towards Saman.

The creature, now the height of three men, floated two meters above the ground, and turned to look at Hank.

"What?" Silver's gruff voice said in unison with Saman's echoing boom, which was tinged with the confused tone of the kid they'd met a few weeks ago.

"The second question," Hank pushed forward, literally and figuratively, shoving Silver to one side and stepping forward, "what would it take for you to not change everything all at once was the second question. Would you agree to bringing back magic?"

Hank paused and let this sink in for both Silver and Saman.

"Would you agree to not free the beings that you feared would end mankind in their anger, jealousy, and vengeance?" She pressed, moving forward and raising her voice at the same time. "Would you instead release their essence, the very energy of who they were, and let it…"

Hank gestured wildly, waving her arms outward in huge circles and then bringing them in as she tried to express the thought of letting the magic sink into the entire world and bring back the wonders of myths and legends that weren't driven by the ego of creatures with an agenda.

Saman read all this in her. She was open now, not fighting him, not blocking him. He could see her from the inside, and knew her delight in learning of the unknown and exploring what could be, what might have been, and what could be. He saw the eternity of hope in her.

Silver pushed his swords back into his sheaths as Saman focused on Hank. Hank would die if this thing attacked her, and Silver was using her as bait, as a distraction, so he could have that one chance to save mankind again.

Silver scaled the Cube of Zoroaster, using the rectangular insets and windows as handholds, leaping from one to the other, making the roof of the building in a matter of moments.

Silver had skills. He had decisiveness based on decades of experience. He knew the odds, and always included the likely math of those in every decision he made in a tight spot. Life was like a poker game, and knowing the odds of how any hand would play out based on how many other players there were and how many cards were left in the deck was the difference between losing everything and winning big.

Drawing his swords, Silver set his feet into a runner's starting position, looking at the finish line that was Saman's back, and tensed to launch himself at his target. He moved forward, the gravel and sand grinding and crunching underfoot, throwing himself into the air between the Cube and Saman.

The huge being was gazing solemnly at Hank, his head hung in contemplation.

Hank slumped, her energy spent, as surely as if she'd wielded her weapons for an hour-long battle. She was exhausted, her mind swimming, and her muscles aching. Her heart sought purchase in her thoughts, unknowing if it had chosen wrong and was poised for breaking, or if it would be uplifted with hope and possibility.

"Magic," Saman vocalized, and waves of energy burst outward from him.

Silver momentum forward, reversed. He flew back, skidding along the top of the Cube to hit the rear parapet, and continuing past it into open air.

If you could see the planet from outer space at that moment, you would have seen an odd atmospheric phenomenon. One single Chinese astronaut did see it, noted it in a notebook using a pencil, because it didn't need gravity to write like a pen, and went on with his duties as all the world, and the future, changed.

The clouds wavered, fluctuating as if something hit them.

People for decades to come would remember that moment. They didn't know why, but they would recall where they were and what they were doing at that precise moment somewhere in the middle of the twenty-first century on a regular October day.

Some would speak of how they knew their best friend, or sister or brother, or their promotion, had just gone through something unexpected.

Some would tell of how their dog or cat or chinchilla stopped and stared at them, and they knew what that little, loved, charmer had wanted.

Some would laugh it off, but knew, without knowing how, that their life had changed forever at that very moment.

Magic had returned to the world.

Hank giggled, then snickered, and then laughed. She felt her own hands on her ribs as her body convulsed. It wasn't funny, but it was a release. It was a bubbling of joy that broke the crust of her being, like a volcano breaking the surface of the earth.

She laughed as this possibility moved outward across the planet. She laughed as Silver was thrown backwards, away from Saman, and continued as he landed in a perfect landing on his feet without any harm, almost a half kilometer away on the asphalt of the parking lot, a meter from the car they'd driven here.

Saman smiled as he looked at her. He felt the possibility of mankind in her laughter. Something he hadn't seen for over two thousand years. This was the thing that was missing. Without mystery, without hope, without possibility, mankind was doomed. But, if you added wonder, if you added magic to the world, then mankind had something more to look forward to.

And it was good.

Epilogue

Silver looked down at Hank, his face creased with concern. He put a hand on each of her shoulders, making her look directly into his eyes.

"Are you sure you want to do this?" Silver asked her.

"Of course I am, silly," Hank bounced up and down on the balls of her feet.

"It means quitting the museum, everything you love."

"Yeah," Hank looked up at Silver, "but don't you get it? Don't you know what I get in place of that, and what all this means?"

Silver stared at her, searching her face, trying to make sure she truly understood the ramifications of the decision.

The moment shattered when a large man approached them on the narrow sidewalk between two buildings.

"An antique store?" Mr. Johns asked, stopping beside them.

The red-faced man wiped his forehead with a handkerchief and took a slurp of his energy drink looking at the sign.

The name of the shop said it all: Silver & Smith Oddities and Antiquities.

A dozen younger people wandered up, all of them greeting Hank with familiarity and affection. One light-skinned black woman glanced appreciatively at Silver.

"He is tall," she nudged Hank with her elbow, "isn't he?"

Silver rolled his eyes, turned, and moved to the shop door. Pulling it open, a brass cowbell clunked clumsily. Silver gestured for Dr. Johns and Hank's friends to enter.

Everyone filed in, chatting, laughing; the friendly mood was infectious.

The museum curator looked around the musty shop, taking in the various oddities and trinkets carefully set on glass cases, acrylic displays, and wooden shelves.

The dark paneling gave a shaded feel to the hole-in-the-wall shop that only had an entry accessible on a side road, almost an alley, in downtown London.

The people wandered through the shop, picking up trinkets and bits and bobs and turning them over in their hands. Curiosity showed on their faces, often accompanied by wonder or amusement.

Silver had already reached out to contacts, as had Hank, and filled the shop quickly enough with trinkets and oddities from around the world.

"Is this what I think it is?" Dr. Johns held up a small jade block. "Is this the He Shi Bi, the Emperor's Lost Seal?"

Silver and Hank looked at him, bemused.

"No, it couldn't be," Johns muttered, setting it back down on a shelf.

"You can't run from your history," Silver leaned on the checkout counter, smiling a contented smile. "It always shows up in the most unexpected, and awkward, ways."

Johns looked at Silver, cocking his head in confusion.

"Are you trying to say something, Silver?" Johns held a red orb in his hand.

Johns had donated the orb since it sat on a shelf in his office for over a decade. It had a vague story, but very little documentation behind the tale. The museum curator had gifted the relic to the two adventurers when they had told him they were opening their shop.

The bell rang and a couple in their forties came in. Hank waved in greeting and the two newcomers nodded and began browsing.

Hank's mates came to the counter, one at a time, each buying some small trinket to show their support, and chatting with her about different things: the coffee shop had expanded its menu, the Cask & Custard Pot had a good playing, and that sort of thing.

Darcy, Hank's roommate, came to the counter. A black cat, Frick, rubbed at her hand as she bought a small brass gong from Thailand.

"They say the gong brings peace if chimed at sunset," Hank said, ringing her up.

"Where's Frack?" Darcy asked.

"Oh, she's here somewhere," Hank waved a hand at the room, "probably on a shelf waiting to hiss at someone."

"I'd like to say I'll miss them," Darcy laughed, "but I'm out so often I barely see my pillow before I'm asleep."

The cowbell over the door clunked its unmelodic music again, and Hank looked up to see an unshaven, older, dour man enter. Glaring around the room, he pulled a flask from the inside pocket of his peacoat and took a long drink from it.

"I got this one," Silver sighed, moving towards the man. "I know him, and no need for anyone else to get their hands dirty with this guy."

The day went along, a handful of curious people coming in, but foot traffic never reached the amount of people as when Hank's friends were in the shop.

The day wore on into evening, and as the beveled glass showed amber rays of a setting sun, the door bonked and clunked again.

A woman shuffled in, turning one eye on the two shopkeepers. She moved to a piano in the shop's front, using various cases and shelves as support.

"Edna," Silver queried, "are you okay?"

Silver hired Edna. He knew they'd be hunting artifacts, and someone had to keep shop while he and Hank were away.

"What?" the woman said, turning and looking at them as if seeing them for the first time. Her glass eye pivoted to follow her real eye. "Oh, you're here. Good to know, good to know. If we had any customers, I'd be working. But I've already dusted all the displays, and I thought I'd play a little Scott Joplin while waiting for some unwitting soul to wander into the shop."

"Okay, Edna," Hank held a cube of platinum and emerald in her hands, having picked it up without realizing it, "you play the piano, and we'll keep ourselves busy."

The room fell silent, except for the pounding of the Maple Leaf Rag as Edna enticed the discordant song of a hundred and twenty-five years ago from the out-of-tune piano. Ragtime required the piano to be tuned to an out-of-tune situation. She'd explained this many times, to Silver's nonchalant agreement and Hank's confusion.

Hank didn't understand how things could work if you set them up to not work. Silver just smiled, and

Hank felt he was laughing at her and her lack of experience in life. As if his smile said that she would understand when she was older.

That was offensive, though, wasn't it? If you couldn't explain it to an intelligent and willing person, wasn't it offensive if you felt they wouldn't understand until they hit some invisible milestone in their future experiences?

After the two had returned from Iran, they didn't talk much about what happened, but they both knew it had changed them—and the world as a whole—more than words could say.

Magic was back.

They didn't know if it had ever existed before anyway. At least, they didn't have any proof.

Hank had talked ad nauseum, for hours on end, about it. She'd discussed, mostly with herself, how it crept into the corners of history and seeped through the cracks of mythology into archeology, sociology, and other sciences that studied ancient cultures. She'd wondered aloud about the chance that there were other sorts of magic, more subtle, that hid in the corners of the mind and in the dark places of society.

Silver stayed silent while Hank expressed these thoughts. He had his own experiences, his own life, and much more than most people would believe, that spoke to this topic. He knew there was more.

But the series of events after leaving his native land and coming here as an ex-pat, arriving and building a life in this place…how it all happened still befuddled him and spoke of greater mysteries.

He knew that Croaker Norge was the equivalent of a travel agent, but Jack Tucker had been the man who had set the plan into motion.

After a series of adventures back home, some with Jack, and meeting Croaker through Jack, Silver came here to escape his past. But in retrospect, perhaps he'd come to embrace it.

"Where do you think he went?" Hank broke into Silver's thoughts with the question.

"Hm?" Silver looked at her. "Who?"

"Saman," she said, "where does a djinni go after returning magic to the world? Did he get a cardphone? Can we call him? Do you think he's watching us?"

"I wouldn't worry about it much." Silver leaned on his elbows on the glass countertop, "he'll show up if he needs to. It really did sound like he wants what's best for the world."

"I know. Weird, right?" Hank tapped a finger on the counter in time to the ancient piano music.

"What's next?" Silver asked, and Hank realized he was looking straight at her.

"Well, with everything that's happened," she said, "we could begin looking for the magic. Seek it out and find it, study how it's cropping up. I wonder if it'll be subtle, or if mythical beasts will just start flocking next week. I bet a lot of the things in museums from ancient cultures might even have power now, like that kukri I touched when I was a kid. Do you think so, Silver?"

"We'll know all that soon enough," he said with a laugh, "but until we do, what's next on the books? Do we have another job, or do I need to call Croaker?"

"Well," Hank pulled out a small notebook, "there is this small country that needs help overthrowing a dictator and mentioned some artifact that empowers the ruler to stay in power…"

Sneak Peek of Silver & Smith and the Doppelganger's Gate

Chapter 1

"I have a plan," Silver said, his brown eyes shifting to Hank and Diana, and he swerved off the road and into the grass and sand beside it.

Silver wore his usual black gear and clothes, a black boonie hat over his smooth, shaved scalp. The buckles and snaps of the various belts, pouches, and straps were his signature polished silver. The cool January morning promised that it would be temperate enough that he wouldn't overheat, even in the desert-like climate.

"But is it a good plan this time?" Hank, sandwiched between Silver and Diana, held her beige boonie hat in place with one hand, and clutched Sydney—her sniper rifle—with the other. "I haven't forgotten what happened when we went to Persia, and really don't want to repeat that."

"Persia is Iran now, and has been for centuries," Silver turned the jeep out of a curve, accelerating across the open plain towards the foothills ahead, "and that wasn't my fault. There was no way I could've known they had a mystical elemental power at their beck and call. But yes, it's a good plan. Do you think these guys'll be able to keep up?"

Hank looked over her shoulder, pushing Diana to one side to see the other all-terrain vehicles carrying the freedom fighters behind them. Her vest and harness jiggled and caught on the leather seat, the equipment in her satchel throwing her off balance.

"Why'd you bring all that stuff?" Silver wiped dust from his face, slowing to enter the foothills. The rebels' vehicles following them were closer.

Hank turned back, rearranging the clattering gear. She glared up at the dark-skinned man, her eyes narrowing.

"Look," Hank's Irish accent came out thicker in short, clipped tones, "you wear blasted black all the time, even out here. I'm wearing beige and browns, and will blend in. You carry the minimal amount, but I carry all kinds of things, because I never know what I'll need. I think it all balances out, don't you?"

Silver shrugged and focused on driving, muttering, "I missed my favorite sci-fi con for this? And it's their golden anniversary, too."

The open-topped jeep bounced between weed-strewn hillocks, its taupe color blending with the terrain, sand flying from under the tires.

A dozen off-road vehicles followed, hot on their tail, swerving around mounds of sand and the tough grass native to the area. Armed men stood in the back of the other jeeps, clutching the roll bar with one arm and automatic rifles with the other. Drones buzzed high overhead, scouting the area and relaying the information to the rebels following Silver and Smith.

The small army of guerillas behind them were allies. The commander of the group hired the duo to help overthrow a petty tyrant and recover a stolen relic.

Diana leaned out the window, pushing her face into the wind. Hank wrapped an arm around her companion to keep her from flying over the short door if the vehicle hit a hummock and took an unexpected bounce. Laughing, Hank tucked her long rifle between her legs with her spare hand, before reaching up and ruffling Diana's ears.

"Does she have to do that?" Silver shouted through the thin black gaiter wrapped over his nose and mouth to keep the dust out.

"You know she loves it," Hank grinned, hooking her hand around Diana's collar.

Diana's tongue lolled, and she raised her nose higher. "She's a dog, and that's what they do."

The German Shepherd turned towards the two of them and wuffed, her ears forward and brow wrinkled.

"We're almost there," Silver said, not taking his eyes off the terrain, "tell me again how Diana's going to find the Mars bracelet."

"It's a cuff, and it's an artifact," Hank clarified, her voice taking on that instructor tone it always did when she explained something, "not a bracelet."

"Looks like a bracelet," Silver said under his breath.

Ignoring him, Hank went on.

"We're looking for a golden cuff, about eight centimeters wide, and with a huge red coral gemstone in the center," Hank gestured, holding her fingers the approximate distance apart as she rattled off the dimensions, "it's etched with the spear and shield symbol of the god Mars, and that's bracketed by an etching of a wolf and woodpecker, both of which were sacred to Mars."

"I know all that," Silver huffed. "I know what we're looking for. I just don't understand how these rebels think some bangle will overthrow General Philonius and his despotic government."

"It's a symbol," Hank said, "and they say the person who has it carries the blessing of Mars. That's the convention of Mars and the rule of law."

"Because the person with it is the strongest," Silver sat up straight, puffing his chest out, his voice matching his posture, "and Mars was the god of war."

"Actually, Mars was thought to originally have been a god of agriculture and the land," Hank gestured towards barren fields in the distance, "and the red coral and gold in the cuff shows the connection to the land, and protecting it and its people. But also, the men behind us probably think that this cuff has magical properties, and with it you have a divine right to rule."

"If that's the case, how come they're trying to overthrow the man who has it instead of just following that divine right thing?" Silver craned his head and slowed to take a tight curve.

"Because the person with it is the strongest," Hank snickered, echoing Silver's own words back to him, "and that makes them have the divine right to rule."

Silver gave her a sidelong glare.

"And where does Diana come into this?" he asked, accelerating, the vehicles behind him roaring around the curve to follow him in ones and twos.

"They say dogs, because of their connection to wolves, can sniff it out," Hank rumpled Diana's fur and spoke in a cutesy voice for the pup's benefit, "as if

Mars himself helps them find the person and item that are best suited to rule together. Yes, he does, doesn't he?"

Diana turned and licked at Hank's face, who squealed and pulled away, laughing.

"Sounds like a bunch of hooey," Silver muttered, "but if the locals think this dog'll help, I'll just have to go with it."

A sandstone wall appeared in the distance, and Silver slowed and turned the jeep behind a hill. When hidden from view, he stopped the jeep, turned it off, and climbed out. The vehicles following them did the same, stopping behind different hills. Men leapt out as the jeeps slowed, hunching as they moved towards Silver and Hank.

The drones above split into smaller groups, some zooming higher into the morning sky, and others breaking off to circle wide around the compound. They'd entered a holding pattern, waiting to be called in for the last part of the plan.

Diana jumped down, glanced at the approaching men, and began sniffing at the ground in a slow circle.

Hank climbed out of the vehicle, arranged her various hanging bags and gear, and pulled her weapon from the seat. When the men came closer, she spoke to them in their language, directing them to positions to keep watch. The men fanned out, a small group staying behind with Hank.

Silver pulled a pair of mini-binoculars from a pouch, dropped to his belly, and crawled to the crest of the hill. The sun was rising behind him and would help hide the group's activities from the sentries. Setting the field glasses to his eyes, he surveilled the compound two kilometers in the distance.

The slightly pinkish stone wall loomed over the sandy ground, the height of five men. Coiled reddish-brown razor wire, looped and tangled, covered the top between thick guard towers; men with rifles paced behind the wire.

The towers rose a couple meters above the wall and tarps provided shade over the sandbag barriers of the corner structures. The tip of a machine gun peeked over the edge of each makeshift nest.

Major Antonio Riva, an olive-skinned man with a thick black moustache, crawled up beside Silver and looked through his own electronic binoculars. The device hummed, recording and transmitting everything it saw to the rebel's base. There, others would dissect the information and feed positions of the enemy back to the rebels making their way to their target.

Riva reached over, poked Silver's arm, and pointed towards the main building.

Silver looked through his binoculars again and focused on where the Major indicated.

Set up in a square with a large courtyard in the middle, the structure had a garden of flowering trees and plants with a fountain in the center. Raising his binoculars higher, Silver focused on the communications array on top of the command building. An a-frame structure of metal pylons supporting various receiving and broadcasting dishes and devices came into focus.

After a few minutes, the two men exchanged looks and nodded. They slid backwards until the enemy guards wouldn't see them, stood, and returned to the others.

"Okay." Silver checked his weapons and pouches, making sure everything was in place. "Our intel was good. The plan stands. Hank, you need to get in close enough to hack their wireless system and take down the electronic defenses. Riva, once Hank signals the all-clear, you take your team and hit them with the main attack on one side, and I'll slip in the secondary door with Diana on the other side. Once in, Diana and I will search out the artifact inside the building and notify you once I have it. With their forces divided and in confusion—and their security systems down—a third assault team will then hit the main gate, which is where we'll gather to make our exit."

Looking around, Silver watched the heads of the men and women nod, their expressions grim. This was the final fight that would determine if they freed their country from a corrupt dictator, or if it wiped away the last vestiges of rebellion.

"Everyone's comms up?" Silver tapped his own earpiece and body cam, then gave a thumbs up.

Everyone mirrored his actions, and they turned and headed towards the compound.

The wall on the other side of the sandstone compound exploded, shaking the ground. Voices shouted and the dunes and grass absorbed the sound of the sharp bark of weapon fire.

The five rebels accompanying Silver were a few meters away, facing outward, hidden and watching for movement.

Silver waited, Diana standing at his feet. The German Shepherd's ears swiveled, following sounds. She raised her nose to scent the air, then lowered it to the ground—walking in a circle around Silver—then into the air again.

Checking his gear one last time, Silver made sure everything was in place. He left his gun strapped into the holster and pulled out two expandable electro-shock batons.

Diana looked at the batons, then up at Silver's face, her head cocked, her forehead wrinkling.

"Less noise," Silver explained to the dog in a whisper, "just a crackle and a soft pop. The gun draws lots more attention. And that means more men, more guns, and more chances of dying. We want to avoid that, right?"

Diana wuffed, watching Silver.

"Glad we agree on that." Silver checked the counter on his cardphone attached to the bracer on his wrist. "Okay, it's about time to go. Look at me, talking to you like you understand every word. Ain't that the damnedest thing?"

The German Shepherd let out a sigh with a huff and turned away to look at the door in the shadowed alcove of the wall.

"We just need to wait for the all-clear from Hank," Silver squatted on his haunches, stroking Diana's neck, "but don't worry, the Hawk has never let me down. She'll get it."

End of Silver & Smith and the Jazeer's Light

253

Enjoying what you're reading?
Want some more for free?

Go to TravisSivart.com/work

Acknowledgments

To everyone who supported me by hanging out while I wrote this on my live twitch stream; Wynn, Gary, Bob, Chris, Sean, Elizabeth, Trin, Eric, and Sandy, as well as those who pushed for more books from me; Jen, Tempe, and Jeanne: my editor Tara for always being encouraging and the best damned wordsmith I know: and, of course, the biggest support in my life, Andrea.

About the Author

Travis I. Sivart writes Fantasy, Science Fiction (including Steampunk, Cyberpunk, Dystopian, & Post-Apocalyptic), Speculative Fiction, Social DIY, and more. You can sometimes find him live-streaming the writing and editing of his latest project from his home in Central Virginia, surrounded by too many cats.

You can find Travis on Amazon, Barnes and Noble, Books-A-Million, and other literary retailers.

Other books by Travis I. Sivart:

<u>Journal of a Stranger, Volume I & II</u>

The thoughts, ideas, philosophies, and inspirations of THE time traveling adventurer, Jack Tucker, delving into the psychology of man, life's eternal questions, burning passions, the quirky pseudo-science of the mind, and more… all while chronicling his own adventures through 70,000 years, past, present, and future.

<u>Harbinger: The Downfall, Book 1</u>

The magical emanations of the comet have brought terrors from the bowels of the earth and increased the powers of necromancy. The chaos above brought out others seeking to wrest control of the land. Five people from different walks of life are thrown together by these events with the knowledge that the world as they know it is ending.

<u>The T.A.L.O.N. Agency:</u>
<u>A Dystopian Superhero Short Story Cycle</u>

Disappear into the shadows of a dark-and-dirty, street-level, borderline cyberpunk dystopian series of stories about heroes and villains, born from one corporation changing the world for the better to create a utopia.

<u>Portals, a Swords & Sorcery Series</u>

Three people disappear from our world and appear in a world of magic and hordes of undead armies. Saving a world that they aren't sure is even real won't be easy.

261

Travis I. Sivart